Part 1

Ac<

19

D1506340

Czechos

1

I turned 22 the week before I rode the train from my home

village to Brno for my final year of Seminary. I had been raised to

Deacon in June, and the summer months had been a welcome rest,

despite the fact that few people outside of my family and close

friends called me by name when they met me in the street. As I

would later become "Father" I was rechristened "Deacon" by the

town.

I rode in the Club Car to escape the noise of children in the

passenger carriage. I sat at a table with a beer and a book, my feet up

on the bench. The lone attendant dozed, and I was content to leave

him to his dreams. The leather of my seat squeaked whenever I

shifted. I opened my book and ignored the blur in the window.

The door to the car opened and the attendant stirred himself

enough to stand behind the bar. A couple came in, unsteady against

the sway of the train, and took the table next to me. I could see their shapes through the frosted glass separating our benches. I tried to concentrate on my book, but the man spoke at an annoyingly loud volume.

"Drinks! We need drinks, before we die of this terrible thirst!"

His Czech bulged with a thick French accent and his vest bulged with his belly. The woman said nothing I could hear. I finished my beer and walked to the bar for another. As I made my way back to my book, the man waved me over. His jacket hung from the hook screwed into the side of the booth, its pockets crammed with papers and magazines.

"Young man! Why are you sitting alone? Did your woman leave you?"

"Not quite. I just wanted a quiet place to read."

"Pah! There is much more to life than just reading."

"As you say, sir. But this is the last chance I will have to read for pleasure. I would like to take advantage of that."

"A student? *Un universitaire*? Will you spend your life with books?"

I inched my way closer to my seat, but I could not bring myself to rudely cut off the conversation.

"Of a sort. I'm in the Seminary."

"Ahh! Bless me, then! I have sinned, and I need all the blessings I can gather."

"I'm not a priest, yet."

"But you will be, and when you are, your blessing will wipe some of the grime from my soul, yes?"

"That isn't how it works. If you will excuse…"

The man waved away my objections.

"A joke, young man. Come. Join us. You will drink a beer, yes? She thinks it is too early to drink."

"Thank you, but I already have one." I raised my glass.

"Join us anyway. I need more stimulating conversation."

I wanted to refuse, but the woman begged me with a look. I slid into the seat next to her.

"Of course. Civilized men need honest conversation."

The man laughed and slapped his hand on the table between us, causing the beer from my glass to slosh over the rim. After I sat, the woman kept her eyes on her hands; her fingers free of rings, the nails torn but clean. I noticed her shoulders were thin and stooped under a too-large, thin coat. Her hair was rough cut, hatless, hacked at her shoulders.

"Are you traveling?"

"We go to Prague. I have a little business, and she is going to work for me."

"What sort of business?"

"I provide entertainment and relaxation for businessmen in the city."

"A health spa? Perhaps a theater?"

"Both. Neither. I provide a service."

I looked at the woman, but she tried to shrink into the corner. She was very pretty, or could have been with a smile. I kept my hands on the table, but I could not stop my fists from clenching.

"You should feel in good company, little priest; even Jesus sat with whores."

"I am not a whore!" She spoke for the first time. Her voice cracked and she squeezed her eyes shut. Every pore oozed defiance, but she did not lift her hands.

"Hush, girl. You need to learn when to speak and when to be silent. What do you think? Will she attract the men? Perhaps you would like to sample her yourself? You're not a priest yet, true?"

"No, I'm not a priest. But I'm afraid I must turn down your most generous offer."

"Is she not beautiful enough for you? Perhaps I should kill her; if she cannot please even one virgin priestling, how can I expect my city gentlemen to want her?"

He reached into his pocket and brought out a razor. He did not open it, but tapped it against the palm of his hand. The woman's eyes grew large and she grabbed at my coat sleeve. I tried to keep my voice calmer than I felt.

"There is no need for dramatics. I suggest you put that away."

"Why?"

"It's making him nervous." I nodded my head toward the porter. "I don't think he wants any stains on his upholstery."

The man stared at me for a long minute, then laughed and put the razor back into his pocket.

"Good joke! I will remember it! Now, about the woman: what if I give you my priestly discount? Half-price for men of the cloth!"

I shook my head and got up from the table. The woman slid over and stood next to me.

"See? She is so excited, she cannot sit still."

"I have to use the…" the woman's voice trailed off.

"Fine. Go. Come back quick. You don't want me to have to look for you."

I slid back into my old seat and picked up my book. The man tried to start a conversation with the porter, who hid behind a newspaper.

I heard the woman return, but did not look for her. The man greeted her.

"There you are. I thought maybe you fell through the hole in the floor and I would have to pay for the railroad to scrape you off the tracks."

She did not reply, but I heard a loud thump, followed by a quieter one. I jumped from my seat and the porter looked up from his newspaper. The woman stood next to the booth, breathing hard. The man still sat, but slumped over with his head on the table. The woman lifted her hand; she had a metal rod clenched in her fist: she had removed the towel bar from the toilet.

I grabbed her wrist before she could swing a second time.

"No, no, no, no. You don't want to do that."

"He is an animal! A sick animal!"

"I know. But the police may not agree with you."

I took the bar from her hand and checked the man. He had a knot on his head, but he breathed.

"He's still alive."

"I should have hit him harder. Give me back the bar and I will do a better job!"

Her eyes scared me. I tossed the rod to the porter and he put it under the bar. I grabbed the woman by the shoulders and shook her.

"Enough! I won't let you kill him. As bad as he is, you don't want that on your soul."

"He is a killer! He told me he kills the girls who don't bring in enough money. He showed me the old blood on his razor."

"Then let me take care of him." I needed to distract her. "Do you have any baggage?"

"Yes. I have a suitcase."

"Go get it."

She looked confused, but followed my directions. When she left the car, I turned to the porter.

"How are you going to handle this?"

The porter studied the man for several minutes and whistled through a missing tooth.

"It seems that sir has had a bit too much brandy to drink. That happens sometimes when a man travels alone. I'm just sorry I was unable to catch him before he fell over the table."

I smiled with him, and helped him lean the man back until he lay supine on the bench, snoring softly. We went through the man's wallet and removed enough for a bottle of brandy. We poured some down his shirt, more in a glass, and spilled some on the table. By the time we finished, the woman returned with a small, battered case.

"What have you done to him?"

I explained the porter's idea.

"But how will that help me?"

"You do not need to stay with him. Do you have any money?"

"No, he said he would pay for everything."

"Well, it sounds to me that he owes you some wages. Do you agree?"

I looked over to the porter. He nodded and smiled. I went back into the man's wallet and removed the rest of his cash, along with the tickets to Prague. I handed them to the woman. Her eyes grew wide and she tried to hand everything back.

"I cannot! It would be stealing!"

"Not really. He promised to pay for your travels, yes? And he intended for you to have housing, yes? Well, this way, he is keeping his promises."

"But I know no one in Prague!"

"Why would you go all the way to Prague? The train stops many times before it arrives there. If you happen to get off to stretch your legs and not make it back on the train in time…"

She started to laugh and threw her arms around me in a quick hug. She tucked the money and tickets into a pocket in her dress and left the car. I did not see her again. I went back to my book. Before long, a conductor came through the car and woke the unconscious man to ask for his ticket. The man, slurring and smelling of liquor, searched his pockets but could only find an empty wallet and his razor. The conductor and the porter grabbed his arms and marched him out of the car as a stowaway. The car finally became quiet, and I was able to enjoy the rest of my journey.

2

I waited for my suitcase near the baggage car. Several men in rail uniforms rushed through the crowd to the back of the train, and I heard a shouted commotion. I found my case among the stack and walked toward the exit. As I stepped up the stairs, a knot of men came close. In the middle, grabbed on all sides, walked the man from the Club Car.

"She robbed me! Her and that bastard priest!"

One of the men tried to calm him down.

"Sir, there were no priests on the train today."

"He didn't look like a…"

He spotted me as I watched.

"It was him! He's the man who robbed me!"

He pulled his arms loose and tried to charge toward me, but the men around him grabbed him and knocked him to the floor. One of the others came up to me.

"Do you know this man, sir?"

"No, but I did see him on the train. He was passed out and smelled like liquor."

The man nodded.

"Yes, that matches our description. We took him to the caboose to try to sober him up, but he tried to cut one of the porters and we had to subdue him. The police will be better able to handle him. Did you happen to see if he had a companion?"

"He was alone when he started the brandy, and he was alone when the conductor found him."

"Thank you, sir. It is sad, when a man cannot handle his drink. Good day."

I climbed the rest of the stairs and came out into daylight.

"If I didn't know better, I'd say that man had some business with you."

I turned to the sound of the voice and saw my friend Vavrinec. He leaned against the fieldstone wall of the station, his cap cocked to one side and a grin on his lips. I walked up to him and shook his hand.

"What man would that be?"

"The one doing all the yelling. I could hear him from out here. Something about a priest…"

"Like the railway man said, there were no priests on that train."

Vavrinec gently punched my shoulder, then put his arm around me and led me from the station. I'd only been away from Brno for a month, but according to Vavrinec, I'd missed the most exciting month of his life. Every detail of the girls he'd kissed, the dances he'd attended, were told with grand gestures. We walked through the streets toward his apartment. I did not need to be at Seminary for a few days.

As we stopped for traffic, I looked at Vavrinec out of the corner of my eye.

"Did you take care of it?"

Vavrinec tried to look innocent.

"Take care of what?"

"'Of what?' My motorcycle! I knew I should have left it with Father Josef."

"It's fine. I haven't even driven it anywhere…much."

"What did you do with it?"

"I met this girl, and she wanted to go for a picnic in the country. My cousin had a sidecar, so…"

"So, you thought you would borrow my motorcycle and go for a drive?"

"Well…yes."

I let him squirm for a few minutes, then slapped his arm.

"That's fine. I figured you would use it."

"You're not mad?"

"Of course not! As long as you cleaned it when you brought it back."

"I knew there was something I meant to do."

We laughed and walked the rest of the way to his apartment.

"Come on. Get cleaned up. We're going to a club tonight."

"I just got here. I don't really feel like going out right away."

"You wouldn't let me take you out to celebrate your Deaconate."

I assumed a lofty expression.

"One does not go out dancing to celebrate such an exalted position."

"Right. So, instead, we are going out to celebrate your arrival."

I shrugged my shoulders.

"Sounds good."

"It will be great! Music, and women, and drinks. We'll really live!"

"I'm supposed to disapprove of those things, you know."

Vavrinec pushed me toward the washbasin.

"Go. Wash. You smell like a train."

3

Vavrinec never just walked; every step bounced, and a straight line was far too constricting for his long legs. His hat sat perpetually crooked, tilted over his right eye.

We spent the evening at a jazz club. Vavrinec seemed to know everyone in the place, and insisted on making me dance with several of the young ladies. One that I danced with wore a cotton dress, white with black dots. Her hair was short and curled towards her chin. We talked as we danced.

"Why would you want to be a priest? Don't you like girls?"

"Of course I like girls. I like you, for instance. But I have to do this for myself."

"I don't understand that. Nobody needs to do anything. My mother thinks I need to settle down and get married, but I want to dance and have fun and see motion pictures and drink wine and watch sunrises and make love. Don't you want to make love?"

I felt my face get hot. "It sounds fun, but my life is on a different path, and that means I have to give up a few things."

"Have you ever even kissed a girl?"

"Yes. I had a sweetheart, back home."

"Did you love her?"

"Sure. But I had to give her up. She's married and has children now."

"That sounds dreadful. I never want to marry!"

"I'm sure you will fall in love one day."

"But what if I fall in love with you? If you're a priest, my heart will break!"

"I doubt that, my dear. You're too delightful to have a broken heart. Besides, we don't even know each other."

I bent down and kissed the tip of her nose, which set her to giggling.

"See? You're far too happy to have a broken heart."

She pouted her lips.

"You're just saying that because you don't love me. Vavrinec, make Jan say he loves me!"

Vavrinec danced over with a giggling, chubby blonde in his arms.

"How could he not love you, dear?"

"I know that, but he says he needs to know a girl before he can love her."

Vavrinec laughed so hard he stopped dancing.

"Dear, I think you are fishing in the wrong river. Jan here is promised to another."

"I know. He told me he's going to be a priest. I don't know how he can give up making love."

Vavrinec switched partners with me.

"Come with me, my dear. Lets find a drink to cheer you up."

The new girl was much shorter and didn't seem interested in talking while we danced. She knew many more dances than I, and tried to lead me in some of the faster steps, but my feet could not keep up.

When the band took a break, she led me to the bar where Vavrinec and my former dance partner waited. Vavrinec put a glass in my hand and turned to the girls.

"Ladies, you are witnessing a very special moment: the last night of freedom for my friend, Jan. Soon, he will lock himself away in the Church. So, tonight, we must show him what he will be missing."

I lifted my drink and swallowed. Only when it was in my throat did I realize Vavrinec had not handed me mild schnapps; the heat rose from my belly to my hair and I bent over in a fit of coughing. Vavrinec laughed and I grabbed his arm. I tried to yell at him, but it came out as a gasp.

"It is a sin to poison a priest!"

"Vodka is a tricky mistress, my friend. You should treat her with more respect."

I sputtered as the girls giggled and pulled us back to the dance floor. We stayed until the band packed their instruments away. One of the girls had an automobile, and Vavrinec drove us out of town to the top of a hill. He and the shorter girl walked over to a thicket, out of sight. The other girl sat next to me, asleep, with her head on my shoulder.

4

For most of the previous 8 years, I had happily slipped into the easy rhythms of Seminary life: classes, masses, my steps set by centuries of tradition. But this year, as we prepared to spend most of our time away from the Seminary, I remembered the feelings of my first day: fear and excitement, and a strong urge to turn around and go back home. I imagined my classmates felt the same. Each term, my class shrank by one or two, as boys decided this life was not for them. A scant dozen remained of a class of more than thirty.

I rode my motorcycle across Brno's narrow, rutted, stone-paved streets to the Seminary dormitories, which sat in the shadow of the Cathedral, high on its hill. I paused in front of the great church; just a few months before, I had received my Deacon's stole in front of the huge altar during the Ordination Rite. The massive stone walls hid a gilded interior, brightened by hours of polishing by younger Seminarians.

I rode the rest of the way to the dormitories and parked the motorcycle next to the garden shed. I had spent enough time, over the past years, tending the vegetable and flower gardens; the brother in charge allowed me a small amount of storage space. I untied my suitcase from the rear fender and covered the machine with a sheet of canvas before I walked through the green mass of cabbages and carrots, peas and potatoes I had planted the spring before.

I smiled at the mass of younger boys clustered near the buildings. The newest boys wore their best clothes from home; more than a few had patches at elbow and knee from previous wearings and wearers. The older boys, those with a few years experience, wore the uniform of black trousers and white shirts. Packed in my case was the cassock I was finally allowed to wear. In the warm sun, I did not envy the priests already wearing theirs.

I found some my classmates and we greeted each other warmly. I listened as they told their stories of the weeks we'd been apart. Damek, an older man who came to the Seminary after his wife died, told about the political tensions of his home near the German border. When my turn came around, I told them about the girl on the train. Miklos, another boy, broke in when I talked about the man's business.

"You mean, she was a fallen woman? And you helped her?"

"What's wrong with that?"

"Women like that are dirty, filthy, sinful creatures."

"Aren't we all?"

"We're supposed to fight against that sort of depravity, Jan. Isn't that what being a priest is all about?"

I thought about my actions on the train.

"I think she did a better job than I did in fighting depravity. That man didn't wake up for over an hour after the lumping she gave his head. Besides, I don't think she had done anything, yet. And, the way she left the train, I doubt she ever will. So, in a sense, she saved her own soul, wouldn't you say?"

Miklos did not answer me. Damek, who had more experience in the world than the rest of us combined, shared a smile with me.

"Was she pretty?"

"Yes. She reminded me a little of a farm girl who came into my father's shop."

"My wife grew up on a farm. The first time I met her, she had a layer of dirt on her face. I didn't recognize her when I saw her clean."

"She was plenty strong, stronger than she looked. I hope she went someplace safe. I know she had enough money."

I finished the story before Miklos spoke again.

"Not only did you associate with a whore, you stole money?"

Before I could answer, a deep, old voice spoke behind me.

"Jan did neither, Miklos. He acted as a priest ought to: he did no violence, and he led a lost soul back to the light. I know a few bishops who could take lessons from him."

I turned to see a short, straight-backed elderly priest, his beard grizzled and snarled in the heat. My smile turned into a grin of pleasure and I clasped his outstretched hand.

"Father Josef! I thought you were going to Switzerland for the year?"

"Fah! The Swiss annoy me. Too polite. Besides, you ruffians need my steadying hand if we're going to make priests of you."

Father Josef grabbed my arm; a habit of his when he wanted someone's attention; the tighter he squeezed, the more important the information. His grip felt like a vise as he pulled me away from the other Deacons.

"Come with me, Jan. I need to talk to you about something."

I left my suitcase and went with him into the small rose garden in the middle of the square formed by the dormitories, classroom building, refectory, and priests' quarters. I joined him and waited. He studied the roses for several minutes before he turned to me.

"Have you given any thought to where you want to go after Seminary?"

I thought for a moment before answering.

"I'd be happy to go anywhere. If I have a choice, some quiet, small village church, like back home. But I will go wherever I am sent."

"You are supposed to visit and work in many churches over the next year. There are few enough of you we can rotate you all around, let you see all sides of the Church."

"'Supposed to?'"

"I want to send you to a special church here in Brno, Jan. It's small, and old; one of the poorest churches in our city."

"This isn't information delicate enough you needed to pull me away. What is going on?"

"What do you know about what has been going on in Germany and Poland?"

"Not very much. I haven't had time for many newspapers lately. Father and I talked about it while I was home, how Hitler wants to build an empire. What does this have to do with my

placement?"

"We are hearing rumors of the German and Polish Jews

being rounded up into ghettos, their movements restricted; of men,

beaten and killed by thugs."

"That's horrible!"

"The church I want to send you to, Jan, is on the edge of our

own Jewish neighborhood."

"Why there? Why me?"

"The story you told about the train helped me make up my

mind. You assessed the situation before you acted. I, we, the Bishop

and I, want to have someone in that area who will think before he

acts."

"Me?"

"Who would you rather we send? Miklos jumps higher than

the Cathedral spires anytime a sin is mentioned, and Damek is too

caught up in the past to pay attention to the present. You're a

thinker. I've watched you play pinochle; you spend as much time

watching everyone else's cards as your own."

"What about the others?"

"They'll make good priests, sure. But you are my best choice."

"What will I have to do?"

"Pay attention. See what happens in the neighborhood."

I sat back on the bench. Father Josef's nervousness made me far more scared than I should have been about a simple church assignment.

"Are you worried that the same things that happened in Germany and Poland are going to happen here?"

"I'm certain they will. I don't know if we will be able to stop them. But neither the Bishop nor I are willing to just let evil happen if we can help it."

"You sound as if this will be a dangerous assignment."

"It might be. Sure, you will learn all the things you would learn in any other church. But I trust you to do more than just learn the rhythms of a parish."

It was my turn to fuss with the roses. I twisted a stem until a thorn poked into my thumb. I sucked the blood and wiped my hand on my leg.

"Alright. I'll go there. Who is the priest? Is it someone I know?"

Father Josef gave the smile of a much younger, clever man.

"Yes, you know him. The Bishop asked me to give up my teaching post and spend some time in a parish. I've agreed."

5

The church looked more like a warehouse than a place of worship. Built of crumbling, smoke-stained bricks, it rose three stories over the shop-lined street that marked a boundary between Jewish and Christian neighborhoods. Men with beards and knotted fringes at their waists and women with their hair covered with kerchiefs shopped alongside men and women in city styles.

I arrived after a two-week stay at the Seminary, where the brothers drilled my classmates and I on what was expected of us. The double doors at the top of the cracked concrete stairs were clean, the brass polished, with lighter patches where generations of hands buffed the metal. I paused at the top and traced my fingers over the intricate doorknobs, on which the image of a cross rose in relief. The crosses tilted away from each other, as if years of use made them too tired to stand upright.

Inside, I found an open doorway leading to the body of the church, and a steep, wooden staircase that turned after a few steps and angled over the entryway. I set my suitcase under the staircase and went through the doorway into the church.

The nave was nothing but a two-storey whitewashed room, with windows on the side not butted up against another building. Rows of wooden chairs ran along the center aisle, the back of each creating a kneeler for the next chair behind it. I ran my hand along the tops as I walked toward the altar. Halfway along the aisle, a circular metal grate set into the floor would provide heat in the winter and treacherous footing for any woman wearing fashionable shoes.

A low communion rail with a hinged gate in the middle separated the nave from the apse. I pushed through and genuflected before I walked around the low, solid altar, covered in a white cloth. Behind, a tiny, gold-covered tabernacle sat on a chest-high pedestal. The key for the lock lay in front of the box. The key was formed in the shape of a cross, the gold rough and dented.

"What do you think?"

I jumped at Father Josef's voice. I hadn't seen him sitting in the last row, in the darkest corner, away from the windows. I walked back to the metal grate and slowly turned in a circle, looking at the Stations mounted along the walls.

"It's beautiful."

"Not quite like the Cathedral. It isn't even really a church. But the old church was falling apart, and this place was available. Someday, the Bishop told me, they will build a new one, but for now…" He spread his arms.

"It doesn't need to be like the Cathedral. I love it! It reminds me of home."

"Are you sure you wouldn't like a bit more gold and jewels?"

I looked around the room.

"No. They would ruin the place."

Father Josef smiled and nodded.

"Good man. Come on; I'll show you where we're staying."

I retrieved my bag from under the stairs and followed Father Josef up to the top floor. Next to the stairs, and cut off from the rest of the floor by a door, were two offices. The top of the desk in one was thick papers and books. A typewriter sat on a side table, the cover the only dusty item in the room. The other office sat empty other than a desk and a chair. Father Josef pointed through the door to the empty office.

"This one is yours. I don't particularly like using mine, and I hate to think of some of our older parishioners climbing the stairs, so

I spend most of my time downstairs in the vestry. You're free to work up here or downstairs."

Father Josef produced a large key and unlocked the door at the back of the short hall.

"Down here is our rectory. It's not much, but the roof doesn't leak."

The rest of the floor had been turned into a large, comfortable apartment. The two bedrooms were close to the door, while the remaining space held a kitchen and living space. The furniture was worn, but solid.

"I hope you're a good cook, Jan; the parish ladies only bring us food twice a week."

I walked through the kitchen and touched the cast-iron cooking pots. My fingers left prints in the dust. I looked over at Father Josef with my eyebrows raised and he gave a bark of laughter.

"There is a decent café down the block. Our stipend will cover meals there if we're careful."

6

Father Josef introduced me to the parish during Sunday

Mass, and I endured the attention. I declined more invitations to

home cooked meals than I accepted, and my presence at someone's

table became a bragging point among the close-knit community.

During the days, Father Josef and I walked the neighborhood,

visiting the homes of the sick and elderly.

One cool afternoon, he led me into the Jewish Quarter.

Before we left the church, we both changed from our cassocks into

secular suits. We moved through the Quarter without attracting

attention. Many shops did brisk business, but a number had boards

nailed across windows and doors. We paused at the end of one street

in front of a storefront that had been gutted by a recent fire, the smell

of smoke still in the air.

"What happened?"

"A few German lads decided to redecorate, it seems. Look

there."

He pointed to the part of the door that remained. Carved into

the wood was the familiar symbol of the swastika. I had seen it in pictures before, but this stood directly in front of me, real in a way a newspaper photograph could never be.

"Why here?"

"I believe this used to be a pawnbroker's shop."

"Is that all? There are three pawnbrokers at the bottom of the Cathedral's hill."

"Let me restate that: this used to be a Jewish pawnbroker. To the Nazis, there's a difference. Come along: we don't want to be late."

"Where are we going?"

Father Josef refused to say anything, and I had to follow him or be left at the sad ruins. We walked for several minutes until he stopped us in front of a plain-looking apartment building. Inside, we walked past the rickety stairs to the back of the building. At the last door, Father Josef knocked lightly. After several minutes, the door creaked open a few inches before being flung open by a shriveled, elderly man.

"Josef! I did not think you were coming."

"Sholem, Abraham."

"And who is that behind you? Wait, come in first; I don't want my neighbors to think I am such a poor host as to leave a friend standing in the hallway. Come! Come!"

When we walked through the door, Father Josef kissed his fingers and touched a small wooden box attached to the lintel. The man, Abraham, shook his head.

"Josef, Josef, Josef. What would your bishop think?"

Father Josef grinned wide.

"Well, we had better not tell him, eh?"

"Of course. Now, who is this strapping young man with you?"

"This is my student, Jan. Jan, may I present Rabbi Abraham Rosenberg, *khazan* of the Skořepka Synagogue, and a devilishly lucky pinochle player."

The old man gave a slight bow towards me.

"Sholem, Jan, student of my old friend, Josef, who is surely a trial sent to test my faith."

Abraham took my arm and led me to the tiny sitting room and indicated I should sit at the table next to the windows that looked over the alley.

"Sit, sit. Friends are a treasure. I will bring tea."

He hurried out of the room, and we heard several bangs from the kitchen. I looked at Father Josef.

"Abraham is an old friend. When I was a little younger than you, one of my Seminary instructors decided we should visit a synagogue. I suppose he wanted us to understand where we came from. It didn't work out so well. A few of the fellows in my class started trying to argue with the elder who had agreed to show us around. They wanted him to admit to…well, I don't even remember what exactly. I just know it didn't make any sense. I tried to quiet them down, but they just yelled louder, until this young man came out to see who was making all that noise. It was Abraham. I'm not sure what he told them, but they quit and left pretty quickly."

"I told them, Josef, if they didn't stop making so much noise while I was trying to study, I was going to stomp them into the ground."

Abraham came back in with a tray of steaming cups. I could smell something flowery and delicious. Father Josef chuckled.

"That's right. I remember now. I couldn't believe this skinny boy thought he could fight two of our boys. So, I went up and stood next to him."

"I still say I didn't need your help."

"I never liked those two anyway. Louts, the both of them!"

"They gave me a headache. I couldn't concentrate for the rest of the day because of all of you."

"You didn't seem very upset about joining us for lunch."

"Of course not; my aunt cooked that day."

I smiled while the two men talked, but I did not want to interrupt. After a while, Father Josef changed the tone.

"Abraham, have you heard anything from Poland?"

"No, nothing. My cousin hasn't written in over a year. I worry about her."

"I do wish you would take my suggestion."

I looked at Father Josef.

"What suggestion?"

But it was Abraham who answered.

"He wants me to run away. Go to England, Switzerland, America."

"And you don't want to?"

Abraham shrugged his thin shoulders.

"My wife is buried here. My parents are buried here. This is my home; I will not leave."

"You're a stubborn old fool, Abraham."

"What sort of life would I have in America, Josef? My friends are here. My life is here. I'm too old to start over. This argument is over, my friend. I was born here. I will die here. Now, let us talk about other things. Tell me, Jan: do you play pinochle?"

Father Josef gave me a wink.

"I've played a few times. My grandfather taught me when I was a child."

"Well, come, sit; we'll take it slow for you until it comes back to you."

We sat around the table and Abraham dealt the cards. I watched the first few hands, not bidding, letting easy tricks go by. I trailed both men after the first round, but I had read their play. Father Josef knew what was coming next. I had told Abraham the truth; my grandfather did teach me to play when I was a child. But I did not mention how Grandfather used his pinochle winnings to pay for his education, beating wealthier students out of their allowances.

As the cards came around again, I caught Father Josef trying not to smile. I took the next two hands with enough points neither man could catch me. Abraham looked very suspicious until Father Josef started laughing.

"Thought to fool an old friend, Josef?"

"Not at all. You were the one who wanted to play cards. It is not my fault Jan is a better player than either of us can hope to be. He spent six weeks on weeding duty in the garden after the other Seminarians complained about him winning all their money."

"I tried to let them win some of it back, but those boys couldn't win if I showed them my hand before I started."

Abraham looked at me for several long seconds before he started to chuckle. Father Josef joined him, and before too long they were back to telling stories of their long friendship.

7

Twice every week, I traveled across the city to the Seminary. I participated in the daily Mass in the Cathedral, helped teach some of the new students, and met with my instructors.

It was during one of these visits that we heard the news of the German Army attack on our border. I was in the middle of a discussion with a few of the newest boys when one of the instructors came into the room and told us to follow him to the dining hall. The cook had a radio, and we listened to the President call for every able-bodied man to prepare for the invasion.

I stood at the back of the room, near the door, so I was one of the few who noticed when Bishop Kupka came into the room. When the reporter started the story over at the beginning, he cleared his throat. The cook turned off the radio.

Bishop Kupka was a very large man. He could make his voice heard from the front of the Cathedral to the back without even trying. I had met him on any number of occasions, usually when I performed a penance cleaning in the Cathedral. He led the Ordination ceremony every summer, and had counseled my classmates and I personally in the weeks leading up to the celebration.

As he stood, he looked over us. I could read the sadness in his eyes. After several long minutes, he spoke.

"Before any of you do anything, come to the Cathedral."

He turned and swept out of the room. The priests gathered at one end of the room, and the rest of us gathered with our friends. Miklos was not present, but Damek and I stood together. He had a look in his eye I had never seen before, and he clenched his fist while mumbling under his breath. I touched his arm and his attention shifted to me.

"I'm going to enlist. I can't let this happen without helping."

I gaped at him. Enlisting had not even occurred to me. I did not want to be a soldier; I certainly did not want to kill anyone.

"What about being a priest?"

"They'll need chaplains. Come with me, Jan."

"But Father Josef…"

"Father Josef will understand. He always taught us to do what was right. Well, this is right."

"They why doesn't it feel right to me?"

Damek gave me a strange look, pity and disbelief, and walked over to the group of priests. I could not hear what they said, but I saw several of them grab his sleeves. He shook off their hands and all but ran out the door.

I wandered through the room and heard the same things from every corner:

"They can't stop us."

"We're joining."

"I'll go."

I walked out the door and started up toward the Cathedral. Halfway there, I noticed everyone else followed me, but nobody walked with me. I felt sick to my stomach; I wondered if I was the only one who did not want to go.

When we entered the Cathedral, we found the Bishop praying in front of the altar. We filed into the front pews and waited while he finished. When he turned to us, his eyes were red-rimmed.

"Boys. My boys. I know what is in your mind. It is in mine as well. How can I protect my home? How can I serve? I cannot answer for you. There is an enemy in this world, and it is impossible for us to ignore the danger to the body. But you must decide if you want to endanger your souls." He did not stand at the lectern, but his voice was the one that reached deaf old men on Sunday morning.

"To kill a man is to take everything from him. It is not an act you will ever forget. As a priest, I have watched many men die. I have held their hands, as they grew cold. I have comforted the living and prayed over the dead."

He paced. He never paced. His shoulders slumped and he sat on the steps that led to the altar.

"Boys, I am not philosophizing. I was in the war. Before I was a priest, I joined my friends. I learned to fight, to kill. No, I learned to butcher; to shred, to rend, in the name of Empire.

"I wasn't one of the crack troops. I wasn't even frontline. I was a guard at a hospital, miles behind the trenches. I had a bed, and a roof, luxuries I never saw because they were there. For months, my life was fifty meters of fence. The only action my rifle saw was a daily cleaning.

"We were too far away to attack, I was sure. I don't think we were really attacked. The man was alone . . . cavalry. He had a lance. I was in the middle of the road, and I forgot I could duck behind a tree when he started charging me. I just lifted up my rifle and fired. I couldn't hit a target during training. I don't know how I hit him. But I did."

I had never seen the Bishop tired. A night of hospital visits, or a Midnight Mass, he always kept going when the rest of us collapsed. Now, he looked older than his years.

"He was dead. He was dead and I killed him. I don't know who he was, where he was from, and I killed him because otherwise he would have killed me.

"That is war, boys. And while I know I cannot stop you from leaving here to fight, I want you to know what war is. It isn't elegant. It isn't a big struggle between two ideologies. It is killing someone because, if you don't, they will kill you."

He had never spoken to us like this. He had been our teacher, our mentor, a provider of ecclesiastic riddles. But now he was just a man, speaking to other men, telling them what he knew. And when he was done, he walked out of the church.

We sat. We talked. I was not the only one to kneel. I prayed for the soldier the Bishop had shot, dead long before I was born; for the Bishop, a man I didn't know as a man.

Half of us made the choice to ride to the enlistment center.
There were few words for us as we left. Some rode in the Bishop's
auto, the rest in the truck the school used for shopping at the market.
The Bishop blessed them as they stood on the steps, then drove
away.

I did not ride with them; but I did travel in the same
direction. I needed to return to my church by nightfall. I rode my
motorcycle slowly through the streets. Everywhere, groups of men
walked together in the same direction. Some carried suitcases; others
had only their clothes.

As I neared the recruitment center, traffic slowed and
vehicles filled the streets. I could barely fit between the stopped cars.
And then, my engine sputtered and died. I pushed the motorcycle off
the road and into an alley before I checked it over. In the confusion
of the day I had forgotten to fill the tank before I left the Seminary. I
cursed my luck and started to push the machine along the side of the
street.

Within a few minutes, I caught up to the boys from the
Seminary. They had all signed their papers and stood in front of the
building, waiting. I stopped to speak to them just as an officer came

out and yelled for their attention. I tried to leave them, but the crowd

was too tight, and I could not push my motorcycle through. When

the officer saw me try, he yelled for soldiers to stop me. He came up

and stood in my way.

"Trying to leave already? You signed up, boy, and you're

going with us. We will use you and your machine."

"But I didn't sign anything!"

The officer waved my objections away, and told the soldiers

to keep near me. One kept a hand on my arm, while the other pushed

my motorcycle.

We were marched to a train that would take us to a camp. I

protested the entire way, but the soldiers wouldn't listen, and none of

the boys spoke up for me. At the train, the soldiers left us. Damek

came up and helped me load the motorcycle into a mostly empty

luggage compartment.

"I knew you would come with us, Jan."

I didn't know what to say to him; he knew I had not

volunteered.

All the Seminarians sat together in one car. I led the younger boys in prayer; some of the other boys in the car who weren't in our group joined us.

The train halted, hours too soon by my watch. The conductor came down the aisle. He told us all to get out. When I asked why, he said the Army was in full retreat and the Government had abandoned Prague. There would be no training, no fighting, no Army for us to join. He looked at me, told me to go home, it was too late. We watched him leave the car and start off across a harvested field.

So, we walked back. I retrieved my motorcycle and pushed it the entire way. The kilometers did not fly beneath us. We found a road to Brno, but discovered it was pointless to ask for a ride from anyone; it was backed up with the autos of people running from the Nazis; it was faster to walk. I did manage to siphon a tankful of fuel from one of the abandoned autos, but I could not bring myself to leave the rest of the boys behind.

We camped one night on the road. None of us had any food, but we found a spring for water and stayed there. Some of the families from the road joined us, but were not willing to share the little food they had, in case they needed it later. It was an odd campsite. One woman was wearing every piece of jewelry she owned, two fur coats, 4 dresses, and carried a suitcase in each hand. She could barely sit down under all that, but she didn't want to give up her things.

We made it back to Brno the next night. At the foot of the Cathedral hill, I left the other boys and drove back to my church. I rode the only moving vehicle.

8

Father Josef and I tried our best to comfort the people of our parish. Daily Mass filled, and the front steps became a social center, as everyone rehashed rumors. I told my story of being kicked off the train over and over, and people asked if I saw this relative or that friend as I walked back to Brno.

Autumn and winter brought new responsibilities to parish work: as the weather cooled, I spent more and more time on my own, visiting those too old or too sick to come to Mass.

German soldiers patrolled the whole city, but the ones near the church spent most of their time watching the Jewish neighborhood. Anyone coming out of the Quarter was stopped and questioned. Father Josef was over two hours late one night when he visited Abraham. Our parishioners stopped visiting Jewish friends; the neighborhood separated.

It wasn't just the German soldiers who changed the city. Gangs of German speaking young men became a common sight on street corners. Any woman walking past was greeted with obscene shouts and rude gestures; any Jewish man could expect shoves and taunts at the very least.

I witnessed many of these attacks at first. I saw men knocked to the ground, and girls stopped and surrounded. By the time I could reach them, the attackers would have wandered away, heads up and faces innocent.

One night in November, I awoke to screams and shattering glass. I stayed in bed for several minutes, convinced I had only heard the sounds in a dream, until someone pounded on the outer door of the apartment. I staggered out in my pants and undershirt and found Father Josef similarly dressed and groggy. He pulled open the door while I shook my head to clear the last remnants of sleep. I didn't see who woke us, but I could hear the cracking voice of a terrified young man.

"Father! You must come! They are killing us!"

Father Josef pulled the boy into the room. He stood nearly as tall as me, and wore a yarmulke.

"Who is killing?"

"Nazis, Father. They're burning everything. You must come. They're burning the synagogue!"

Father Josef looked at me and I watched the blood drain as quickly from his face as I could feel in my own. I spoke first.

"The synagogue…"

"Abraham…"

I ducked into my room and jammed my feet into my shoes. I grabbed my jacket and was back before Father Josef. He stuck his head out.

"Go, Jan. I'll catch up."

My heart thudded against my ribs as I reached the front door. The boy tried to come with me, but I gently pushed him back toward the stairs.

"Stay here. You'll be safe."

I didn't wait to see if he listened.

Outside, burning buildings illuminated the world. People who lived along the street came out of their apartments in their robes and pajamas, coats and shoes thrown on in haste. I didn't stop to talk to anyone but ran in the direction of the synagogue.

I didn't see the streets I ran through; I didn't hear the crunch of glass under my feet. I only slowed when I reached the synagogue's block. Men in uniform and civilian clothes clogged the street. I could see hastily made clubs in many fists. They all watched as those in the front of the crowd pried up bricks from the street to hurl at the windows.

I shoved my way through. I spoke German, but I didn't bother trying to understand the growls of those I jostled. As I came to the front, two soldiers lit torches and started up the steps. My screams were mostly lost in the cheers of the crowd.

"Stop! What are you doing?"

The people around me heard me, and two of them grabbed my arms.

"Are you a Jew? Are you a Jew?"

I could smell the beer on their breath. I shook my head, but they didn't let me go. As the building caught flame, the front door opened and Abraham staggered out, his arms full with a large wooden chest. He made it down the steps before the soldiers grabbed him. They knocked the chest out his arms and it splintered on the ground. I heard Abraham shriek as a large scroll rolled onto the ground. He stooped to pick it up and the soldiers shoved him over. I shook off the hands holding me and rushed forward.

"Leave him alone!"

I couldn't reach Abraham. The soldiers circled around him. I saw the first boot strike his head. Blood dribbled from his nose, black in the flickering light. The fire in the synagogue grew to a solid wall of flames, and all the men became shadows, except for Abraham. I saw him try to push himself up to his knees, but they wouldn't hold him. He pulled himself on the ground until he reached the scroll. He rolled onto his back, the scroll clutched to his breast. More boots.

"No! Abraham!"

I screamed, but I couldn't hear myself. The only sound was my pulse. Hands grabbed at me and threw me to the ground. I rolled to my side and could see Abraham's face through the legs. His eyes met mine. He could see me, but I could not reach him. He tried to push the scroll toward me, but one of the soldiers snatched it from his hands and threw it into the fire.

I wanted to close my eyes. I felt a boot against my own ribs. But I could not let that brave old man die alone. I held his gaze until the light left his eyes.

He died long before they stopped beating him.

I was dragged to my feet and the soldiers pushed me in front of a young officer. He spoke to me in German.

"Who are you?"

I pretended I didn't understand him. His gloved hand grabbed my jaw and he shoved my face to the side. He studied my profile for a moment, then let go.

"You don't look like a Jew. What are you doing here?"

I still didn't answer. I could hear a commotion behind me and a familiar voice yelled out.

"He's with me. He's my deacon. Please, let me take him home."

Father Josef, dressed in his cassock, pushed through the last of the crowd and stood just outside the ring of soldiers.

"Please. He's just a boy. Let him go."

The officer looked me in the eye and spoke in heavily accented Czech.

"You're a deacon?"

I nodded. He motioned to the soldiers to let me go. I slumped, but did not let myself fall to the ground.

"We're not after Catholics tonight."

He signaled and the soldiers marched down the street. The drunken crowd followed them. Father Josef grabbed my arms and held me up until the last of them went around the corner. I wept and sank to my knees. He left me and walked slowly to his friend.

"Oh, Abraham. What have they done to you?" He knelt. I crawled over to the two of them.

"I … I couldn't stop them. They beat…"

"Shh. I know, lad. I know."

We stayed next to Abraham for a long time. When I could stand, we picked up his body and walked down the street to his apartment. The doors stood open, and the lowest windows of the building had all been broken. Inside the apartment, books and paintings lay broken on the floor. We put Abraham on his bed and wrapped him in a clean sheet. I started to kneel, but Father Josef stopped me.

"No. We do it his way."

He started to chant in a language I didn't know. I bowed my head and listened. When he finished, he turned and walked out of the room.

9

I found broken glass in strange places, far away from the destroyed buildings, for months. Soldiers kept our parishioners out of the neighborhoods, but anyone who walked through the streets picked up shards in their shoes. I swept the church every day, and the sight of those little bits of glass kept the horror fresh in my mind.

We did not know how many more people died; I saw only Abraham. But the rumors spoke of dozens, maybe hundreds more. I could not forget the look in Abraham's eyes as he died. Anytime I was alone, I felt him watching me, pleading for help. More nights than I could count, those demanding eyes woke me.

Father Josef tried to control the grief and anger over his friend as we prepared for the Christmas season, but I could see the fire in his soul. I felt it in my own. We took, independently, to walking along the unofficial border around the Quarter. German patrols came and went, but our collars kept us fairly unmolested.

The first snow of the season brought a welcome mask to the debris in the nearby streets. It also brought Vavrinec back into my life. He found me in the church one afternoon as I changed the altar candles. I had my back to the door when he came in.

"You know, I never thought I would say this, but you look right up there."

I turned to his voice and knocked the box of candles off the altar. When I saw who it was, I ignored the mess and jumped over the communion rail to greet him.

"Where have you been? I haven't seen you in months."

"Oh, here and there. I spent a few weeks in Prague."

"In Prague?"

"Well, near there. Someone thought I should be in the Army. I disagreed with them; particularly when I found out they wanted me to use a pistol to fight tanks. After my commanding officer ran off and hid in a cellar, I decided the civilian life was more to my liking."

"It sounds like your military career went about as well as mine."

"Your military career?"

We sat in the last row and I told him about my aborted train journey towards the battle. He found much more amusement in my situation than I had at the time. Then he told me how he had returned to Brno to find a letter from his parents, left with a neighbor, telling him they had escaped to Switzerland before the Germans reached the city.

"Why didn't you go, too?"

"By the time I got the letter, they'd set up travel restrictions. At least I know they're safe. That was about two weeks ago. I left Prague after the burning."

"The burning?"

"The Nazis went in and destroyed most of the Jewish areas of Prague."

I sat back, stunned.

"It happened there, too?"

Vavrinec shook his head. He suddenly looked very tired.

"It happened everywhere. Everywhere the Germans are, anyway."

"My God…"

"On the day I left, I saw soldiers herding people to the train station. I couldn't get close enough to be sure, but I think they were all Jews."

I closed my eyes and put my head in my hands.

"Why are they doing this?"

"I don't know, Jan. But I'm scared."

We sat for a long time without talking. I'd never known Vavrinec to go so long without laughter or a joke. It pained me to see my friend look so serious.

10

Christmas came and went with little of the normal fanfare. Father Josef kept the parish organized and busy, making and collecting food for our Jewish neighbors. But when we tried to deliver it, the soldiers confiscated everything, including the wagon.

In February, I was given leave to visit my family for a few weeks. When I returned, the Seminary was a mass of confusion and rumor. I had not seen a newspaper while I was home, so I was surprised to learn the Pope had died. According to the younger students, he died six different ways, except he hadn't actually died but had been kidnapped by Chinese spies.

I did not put much trust in the rumors. But I did hear the Bishop planned to take Seminarians to Rome for the Conclave to elect a new Pope.

As I made my way from the Seminary to my church, I was torn. I wanted to see the Conclave, and the instructor I spoke with assured me I was welcome to come along. But, with all the pain and suffering around the city, I didn't feel right about going to such a celebration.

When I arrived at the warehouse church, I found Father Josef coming out of the makeshift Confessional, which had started life as a large storage closet, his eyes drawn. He greeted me warmly and led me up to the apartment. His eyes looked everywhere but at me as I explained my conundrum. After a few minutes, he stopped me.

"They're gone, Jan."

"Who are gone?"

"The Jews. While you were home. The Germans rounded them up like sheep, marched them through town, and put them on a train. They're gone."

"Just like in Prague…where are they taking them?"

"I don't know. The train started off east, but they could be anywhere by now."

"Can we find them?"

"And do what? Rescue them?"

I didn't know what to say. Part of me wanted to ride off to the rescue. I'd seen some American cowboy films. I pictured myself on my motorcycle, leading them home. When I looked up, I could see my youth reflected in Father Josef's eyes.

"There isn't anything you or I can do, Jan. Not here. Not now."

"So what do we do? What do I do?"

"That is an easy question to answer: you go to Rome."

"How can I go to Rome at a time like this?"

"This is the time we live in. This is the opportunity you have, and it may never come again for you. The whole seminary is going; this is part of your education, and you need to see it. I'll stay here. You need to go. I'll still be here when you get back."

"Are you sure?"

He handed me an envelope.

"What's this?"

"I have a friend at the American college. If you have the chance, give him this: it is everything that has gone on in Brno since the Nazis came. Tell him what you've seen. He may be able to help."

I knew he was right. I knew I might never have another chance to do some good to protect innocents.

11

3 March 1939

Dear Mother and Father,

Pacis Exsisto Vobis

It is 0300, and Rome is still celebrating. "On the second day

of the Conclave, by nearly unanimous consent, Eugenio Maria

Giuseppe Giovanni, Cardinal Pacelli, the Cardinal Secretary of State,

became Pope," according to the German language newspaper.

I've have had a wonderful time in Rome. We have been

staying at the American College, since Czechoslovakia does not

have its own, and the Bishop refuses to interact with the Germans.

They have been such wonderful hosts, and I have made many new

friends. One in particular, a young priest named Father Robert

Banich, has been taking me around the city to see all his favorite

spots. His grandmother was a Czech, and he remembered enough of

her language that we could talk.

It has surprised me that we have not gone to very many

Cathedrals or palaces. Instead, we have been to many tiny

neighborhood churches, tucked back away from the crowds and

foreign visitors. It was in these tiny churches, with their faded carpets and unpadded pews, that I felt the most comfortable. There is a joyful nearness to God in the simplicity that cannot happen in the huge works of art people have created in His name. I remember old Father Petr telling me when I was little that the Mass is when we invite God to join us in a meal together. These churches feel like mother's kitchen. I could imagine one of the chipped statues of the Child Jesus sneaking a sweet from the table with a giggle here.

I saw St. Peter's Basilica, but it was so overwhelming, so huge, so absolutely beyond what I could comprehend. I used to think the Cathedral in Brno was huge. Here, I felt lost. I could never be one of those bureaucratic priests. I have no ambition to be that far separated from the world.

They remind me of elegantly dressed monks, going about their daily tasks. But instead of tending flocks and caring for gardens, they spend their days chasing bits of paper and jockeying for position and power. It is hard to believe that the little tattered church, where my friend Robert brings them the wine they cannot buy for themselves, is the same Church as the huge marble halls filled with bejeweled men in silk cassocks.

The Conclave has been amazing. For two days the square was packed with people from all over the world. We tried to stay together, but with so many people moving around the Square, we were gradually separated. In the evenings, we would discuss the rumors that we heard from different parts of the crowd. I stayed with Robert as much as possible, and between the two of us, we could usually find someone who shared a common language with us.

Everyone heard different stories of who the favorites of the Conclave were, and one of my classmates even came across a nun who was taking bets on the outcome. I don't know if I believe him. The most common name Robert and I heard the first day was a Cardinal Schulte, but neither of us knew anything about him. The next day, we didn't hear his name once.

A Conclave is not a quiet, solemn affair out in the Square. You should have seen the crowd the first time the smoke came out. Some people were jumping or crying. I could not hear Robert at all for the noise, and he was right beside me. I think many people were disappointed, but not surprised, that the first votes didn't result in white smoke.

After that, the Square cleared out a little as people left for a quick midday meal. I made my way over to where a priest was telling a group of young people a story. Robert went with me and translated for me. He was telling about how, centuries ago, the citizens of Rome would wait in the square for the new Pope to appear. If they didn't like the man chosen, they would boo and the Cardinals would go back and try again.

The afternoon votes went the same way. Twice more, black smoke came from the Sistine Chapel. After the second time, most of the crowd drifted away. We went back to our temporary home to nap before a startlingly tasty late evening meal of something called *calamari*. No one would tell me what it was, but I liked it. Robert took me to see the Spanish Steps, where we saw three young women beat a man. When I started to intervene, Robert stopped me, saying the man probably deserved what he got.

Day two started very bright. We think the sun shines brightly at home, but it is nothing compared to here. We joined together for Mass, and prayed for wisdom for the Cardinals. As we left, one of the other boys from home said he had heard today was one of the Cardinal's birthday, and wondered how many votes he would get as birthday presents. This earned him a cuff to the head by one of the American priests and a penance by the Bishop.

I am afraid I was confused on the voting today. Some people were claiming that we had a Pope after one afternoon vote, while others said it took two. I don't know how they could tell, since we were all outside. All I know for certain is, the last smoke we saw came out first white, then black, then grey. Someone finally addressed the people and announced who the new Pope was and gave us his name:

Pius XII.

We waited to be addressed by His Holiness. After a time, we finally caught a glimpse of him. I was close enough to see that he was a thin, serious-faced man with large glasses. But when he smiled, there was a kindness in him that warmed me. I think he will be a good Pope, but I fear he will have his hands full very soon.

Tomorrow we will make arrangements to come home. We will not be able to stay for the actual coronation, but none of us feel like we are missing anything after the last few days. Rome is exciting, but I do not belong here. I will be glad to see our hills as spring arrives. I will let you know when I have made it back to Brno. I have presents for all of you.

I think it is time to go to sleep. The city will party all night long, but, as I said before, I am not of the city.

Love,

J.

12

I could not tell my parents everything about Rome.

While we waited between votes, I showed Robert the envelope Father Josef had given to me before I left Brno. When he saw the name, his eyes grew wide.

"Yes, I know him. But you can't go talk to him until after the Conclave."

"Why not?"

"Because, two months ago, he became the Cardinal Archbishop of Boston's personal aide. He's in charge while the Cardinal is in Conclave, and will not be available until the voting is done."

I spent the next three days with a knot in my stomach. I tried to hide it from Robert as he led me around the city. I really did enjoy the small, worn, old churches, but my mind focused on the folded letter from Father Josef. I kept it in my pocket at all times. I knew what it said, and I was terrified I would lose it. Finally, Robert was able to arrange a meeting, and he accompanied me to the antechamber of the Cardinal's temporary offices.

The door opened and Robert gestured me in. Because I spoke no English, Robert would translate for us. It made for a very slow conversation.

The priest who sat behind the desk came from the same generation as Father Josef, but he looked ten years younger. A wiry man with intelligent eyes, he said nothing as Robert introduced me and I handed him the letter from Father Josef. He read with small pair of glasses on the end of his long nose. When he finished, he folded the letter back into the envelope. He set it on the desk and leaned back in his chair with his eyes closed. I shifted back and forth on my feet while I waited.

When he spoke, he surprised both Robert and me by speaking in Czech.

"Is all of this true? Is it as Josef said?"

"Yes. We saw the soldiers do the burning."

"And you're sure they were not acting in self defense?"

"They kicked an old man to death. He could barely walk up and down the stairs to his synagogue on the best days."

The man got up and walked over to the window at the back of the office. He stood for a very long time, his hands clasped behind his back. I don't know if he saw the city on the other side of the

pane. He didn't turn around again when he spoke, and the only

English words I caught were Robert's name and the word "coffee."

Robert bowed and hurried out of the room. Only when the door

closed did he turn to face me again.

"It was Jan, yes? Your name? Jan, we knew about this. It did

not just happen in Czechoslovakia. In Germany, we think all

synagogues have been destroyed. The German government claims

loyal German citizens, outraged over the assassination of some

diplomat, did this. And we have no proof otherwise."

"But I saw…"

"I know what you saw. Josef spelled it out very clearly. But

did you hear anyone give any reason for it?"

"I didn't hear anything. They beat me as well."

"Yes. I'm sorry about that. Were you badly hurt?"

"No. I lived."

He looked back out the window. Robert returned with a tray

and two cups of coffee. Without a word, he placed the tray on the

desk and left again. The priest returned to the desk and sat. He gestured me to the chair opposite him. He placed a cup in front of both of us.

"Father, the church must…"

"The church. The church cannot do anything, my boy. Do you know what has been going on in Italy?"

I shook my head.

"The church must be as cautious here as Czechs must be when surrounded by Germans. The Italian government is allied to Germany, and we are defenseless here."

"Surely the government would not move against the church."

He sighed.

"We cannot take that chance. We are balanced over a sword here, Jan."

"What about America? You'll be back in America soon, yes? Can you not tell your leaders?"

"If we know, they know, too. And they'll have the same answer: we don't want another Great War. They want to contain Hitler, not confront him."

"People are dying!"

He slammed his hand on the top of the desk so hard the coffee sloshed from my cup. I jumped back in my seat. His eyes flashed with sudden anger.

"Do you think I don't know that? You saw one man die; we think the Germans have killed thousands. We can't do anything about it! Do you understand?"

"You can tell the world."

He sat back. The anger flowed out of him and his shoulders slumped. He suddenly looked far older than Father Josef.

"Tell them what? That people half a world away are having a difficult time, but we have no proof? The last ten years have been difficult for everyone; how would you have me convince people?"

"Tell them the truth. They must believe the truth."

"The truth? Truth is a weak weapon."

He stood up and led me to the door. He paused with his hand on the handle.

"I'm sorry I don't have better answers for you, Jan. Please, tell Josef I'm sorry. I'm sorry."

He opened the door and ushered me out.

The next day, we returned to Czechoslovakia.

13

When I returned to Brno, I told Father Josef about my meeting with his friend in Rome. He tried to hide his disappointment, but I could tell his friend's response hurt him.

As the weather warmed, I began a new part of my Seminary activities. I had spent all of my time in either the little warehouse church or in the Cathedral. Even with all the upset in the country, part of my education required me to travel around and see how other churches worked. With my motorcycle, I could travel further than some of my classmates, so I spent April and May moving from one country church to the next. I met many good, scared people.

One afternoon, as I rode back toward Brno after a week in a village to the south, I came across an abandoned Gypsy camp.

I rode along the river when I found a dozen or so carts pulled off the road in an unplanted field. They were in a circle, tongue to axle, and wash lines half-full of laundry were strung where they could catch the breeze. Most of the carts showed remnants of once bright paint, reds and yellows, flowers and vines. From the road, everything looked as it should.

It was the silence that did not belong. Nothing living moved; no birds in the trees, no insects around my head. No people, no horses; just tracks through the grass, pointed north. There was no smell of food or fire, no sound. Even the laundry, long dried, hung limp. The emptiness of the place gripped my bowels. Something terrible had happened, but I did not want to know what. My instincts told me to leave, to run, to get back on my motorcycle and drive away as fast as possible.

I couldn't leave. I was not brave, but I could not leave without looking. As I came closer into the camp, I saw many objects, things left behind, dropped in a mad rush. A half-finished sock, with a long loose thread, sat next to a squashed ball of red yarn; an iron striker and a worn chunk of flint were half covered in dust next to the stone fire circle; a pair of brightly dressed dolls lay facedown next to the steps to one wagon. I picked one up and felt the silk of its tiny scarf. This doll had been treasured.

My hands shook as I went from place to place, object to object. All of them were valuable, not to be left behind. At one edge of the camp, I came across a pair of tracks made by rubber tires. The wagons all had wooden wheels with iron rims. I couldn't find

anything else around the outside of the camp. I steeled myself and
moved on to the carts.

The first cart I checked had to belong to the leader. Large
enough for a railed porch on the rear, it held the most color of any.
The door was open, so I felt less like an intruder. I did not go in, but
simply peeked my head under the lintel. Everything was neatly
puzzled away, either freshly packed or not yet removed for the night.
There was little enough room for anyone to come in, yet someone
must have ridden in the back. There was one chair set upright next to
the door, a child's chair, a princess' chair, padded. A carved toy
horse sat precisely in the middle, left waiting for her mistress to
return.

The next cart yielded even less. It was set up for the night,
bed across the floor, but only clothes filled the spaces. I searched
each cart and found nothing to tell me what happened.

Except for the last cart. It sat in the middle, but I had left it
for last for a reason. Tied to the axle was the only living creature
around. A dog; a very hungry dog, to judge by his reaction to me. He
jumped and snarled when I touched his cart. I hadn't seen him as I
walked through the camp because of the shadow under the cart. The

thick leather thong that secured him showed signs of gnawing, but he had not broken free yet, and might not in his condition. I had my grandfather's old knife in my pocket, and my lunch was still in my saddlebags. Since he wouldn't let me near the cart, I decided bribery would be a minor sin.

The poor beast ripped my bread to shreds in a heartbeat, and I barely had time to slide the blade through the leather near his head before he tried to bite me. I ran and jumped into a low-hanging branch. He chased me until he came to the point where he would have been jerked back, where he stopped. He took a few steps beyond his old boundary, then ran off in the direction the horse tracks led.

The last cart stood before me. It was no different on the outside from most of the others. The doors and window were closed, but so were several of the others. I tried to open the door. It took me several minutes to find it had been nailed shut. I had seen several hammers around the camp, so it was only the work of a minute to pull the nails from the door. As the last one came loose, a foul odor crawled out.

I hadn't been alone in the camp. I had only been the last living person. The man on the bed was ancient, wrinkled and bald. His skin was a waxy yellow and his mouth hinged open in a gasp he couldn't complete. He was dressed in a long white shirt, and I could see no wounds. I didn't come inside to check closely.

I staggered out into the camp before I vomited. Where the dog had sat guard, I knelt until I stopped trembling. It was all I could do to close the door of the cart again. The nails I pulled were where I had dropped them. I did not replace them.

14

Father Josef had worked as a missionary in Africa. He did not tell stories about his time there, just that he had seen the very worst in humanity. When I told him about the Gypsy camp, I could see the memory of past pain in his eyes; they mirrored my own.

For the rest of the spring, even while I traveled around the city and learned all I could, I could not concentrate on my vocation. I tried not to let it show, but after Rome and the Gypsy camp, I started to seriously doubt whether I would be able to do any good as a priest. I hadn't been able to stop any of the evil I saw, and I couldn't rely on the Church leaders to help me.

As my deaconate came closer to an end, I struggled with my choices. I tried to talk to Father Josef about it, but he told me I needed to work through my problems myself; he could not tell me what to do. During my last month, I went to the Cathedral to talk to the Bishop about my questions.

"What does your heart tell you, Jan? What is the right thing for you to do?"

"I don't know."

"You've seen some of the worst in the Church. There are those who think the survival of the church trumps all other considerations. They're willing to sacrifice the lives of individuals to keep the institution safe."

"But these are people. Don't people matter more?"

"They should; without people, there is no church. It doesn't matter if they're Catholic or not. But it can be hard to see the people from the top of a tower. And that's where the decisions are made."

"I don't know if I can do this. I need time to think."

"I cannot force you to do anything, Jan. Officially, you're ready to be a priest. Josef has told me he sees strong potential in you. I know you have your convictions; let those lead you. Go: visit your family. Talk to those you trust. You will find the answer that is right for you."

15

My family had lived in the same village for generations. My great-grandfather had opened a sawmill that supplied materials to the railroad. When the rail spur through the town finished, my grandfather became a broker between local farmers and city markets. My father continued the business, but also opened a shop for the goods that came in to the village. From the time I grew tall enough to reach the till, I worked in the shop after school, and when I returned from Brno I quickly found myself behind the counter.

After two weeks of working in the shop, spending evenings with my family, I had decided to return to Brno for ordination. Father and Mother told me they would support my decision, no matter what it was; my younger sister, Ryba, wanted me to stay in the village, but told me she could see the desire to be a priest in my eyes. My sister always looked beyond the surface.

On the day I planned to return to Brno, a letter arrived for me from Father Josef:

Jan,

I'm afraid your decision is no longer in your own hands. The seminary has been closed and the Bishop is under house arrest. Most of the other students were arrested and questioned. They beat

Damek badly. He said they asked him about a Gypsy camp. I think

they are looking for you.

You need to stay where you are, Jan. Don't try to contact me,

or any of us.

Josef

I sat on my bed for a long time, looking at that letter; my

friends had been hurt because of me. My eyes burned. They

shouldn't have to suffer because of me, because of something I saw.

I wanted to rush back to Brno, to turn myself in, to fix the wrong.

I stayed in my room long enough my parents came to look

for me. I showed them the letter.

"I'm the one they were looking for."

Father put his hand on my shoulder.

"There isn't anything you can do."

"But my friends…"

"Your friends are alive."

"It should be me, not them. If I hadn't run away…"

Mother sat on my bed next to me.

"You didn't run away, Jan."

"It still should have been me. I need to go back there."

"And do what? Can you heal their hurts? Can you change the past? Would your friends want you to put yourself in harm's way?" Father had a way of asking questions to clear my head.

"No, but…"

"No, Jan. The situation is what it is; you cannot change it. Don't waste their sacrifice."

I knew he was right. I put my head in my hands and wept for my friends. Mother put her arm around me and I became the little boy I had been, looking for the healing only a mother can give.

When I sat up again, I thought about the other part of the letter.

"I can't be a priest."

Mother had the right words this time.

"If it is still something you want, don't surrender just yet. You will find a way."

"And what do I do while I wait?"

"Stay here; work with Father; try to find some peace. You've had a very difficult year, Jan. You need to heal, too."

So I stayed. I worked in the store. I reconnected with my old friends and readjusted to the slow rhythm of the village. I should have known peace would not last.

German soldiers overwhelmed Brno almost immediately after they crossed the borders. They covered the main roads, rails, and cities, but largely left the villages alone. Father told me they had seen several troop trains and vehicle convoys, but few had stopped in the village. We were simply too small to bother with.

I heard the sirens long before the first motorcycle stopped in the village square, and a crowd gathered by the time the last truck, of three, ground to a halt. Soldiers hopped out of the trucks and stretched before shouldering their rifles and advancing toward the crowd.

A staff car followed the motorcycles, and when the soldiers had stopped in front of us, a tall, young officer stepped out. He wore a long, black leather coat over a grey uniform, different from the green uniforms I used to see in Brno. He held a riding crop in one hand and a pair of gloves in the other. It was too warm for the coat, but he did not make any move to remove it. As he came closer, I could see he wore a thin blonde mustache. As he walked he slapped the riding crop against his leg.

He looked us over for several minutes, walking slowly up and down behind the line of his own men. On his own, he would have looked like someone's little brother, dressed up in a uniform too old for him; with his troops, he became frightening.

Finally, he spoke in heavily accented Czech.

"Is there anyone who speaks German?"

Everyone looked around. I lifted my hand and the soldiers brought me over to speak to the officer.

"You will translate for me. Who is in charge here?"

"The mayor."

"Where is he?"

I pointed to the mayor, an elderly man who ran a barbershop until his eyesight became so bad he couldn't tell the difference between an ear and a clump of hair. He was elected mayor because everyone liked him. The soldiers grabbed him and pulled him forward.

"You are the mayor?"

"Yes, sir."

"You will answer my questions. Are there any factories around here?"

"No, sir. Only farms."

"Farms? What do you grow?"

"Potatoes, sir. Turnips. Some wheat. Some sheep."

"But no factories?"

"No, sir."

"What about the trees? Is there a sawmill here?"

"Not since I was a boy."

"This won't do at all. You may go."

The mayor stepped back. I moved to go with him, but the officer shook his head.

"We need provisions. We will resupply here."

"My father owns the only shop that sells food."

"You will take me there."

I walked with the officer and several soldiers to the shop. The soldiers filled boxes with all the canned goods I had. They piled them by the door, then went back for the bags of flour and coffee. While they worked, the officer walked up and down the aisle of clothes and household goods. He did not touch anything. He came up to the counter where I was trying to write down everything the soldiers took from the shelves.

"You would know this: are there any Jews in this village?"

"None."

"Are you sure? Sometimes they hide themselves, pretend to be people."

"I don't know of anyone who could possibly be Jewish."

He did not look like he believed me.

"We will see."

He walked out the door. A large soldier, older than most of the others, came back to the counter with a briefcase in his hand. He set it on the counter and pulled out a document. In blocky handwriting, and with his tongue caught between his teeth, he laboriously filled out the document.

"This will allow you to draw money for the food from the government. Just take it to your district Reich office, and they will pay you."

"How much will they pay me?"

He blinked at me, then thrust the document at me, closed his briefcase, and walked out the door. I read through it; we would receive, if the paper were honored, less than half the value of the goods.

I heard the officer speaking in German out in the square. I caught the word "Jews" and "lies." I rushed out to see soldiers pulling the new schoolteacher from the crowd. He arrived in the village after I left for Seminary, and I hadn't met him personally yet. When the officer spotted me, he gestured for the soldiers to let me through.

"Do you know this man?"

"He's our schoolteacher."

"Is he from around here?"

I opened my mouth, but didn't say anything. I didn't know what would happen. If I said yes, someone might give away the lie; if I said no, I couldn't tell what the Nazi officer would do.

He asked again.

"Is he from this village? Answer me!"

I still didn't say anything. The officer nodded his head thoughtfully.

"He's not, is he? He's a stranger here."

I finally found my voice.

"He's lived here for years."

"But where did he come from. Do you know? I think he is hiding something. He will come with us." The officer turned to the men holding the teacher.

"Put him in the truck and mount your vehicles."

Soldiers grabbed the schoolteacher's arms and pulled him to the truck. The slight man couldn't even fight back. They lifted him bodily off the ground and all but threw him into the truck. The motorcyclists kicked their machines to life as the soldiers took their places, then led the convoy out of the village with the scream of their sirens. The crowd stood in place until the vehicles were out of sight.

Many people asked me what had happened. I couldn't explain it. I did not know why they had grabbed the schoolteacher. He looked like anyone else, and when someone said his name, it was a common Czech surname.

When Father came to the shop, I told him what happened. When I told him about the schoolteacher, his face paled. He sank into his chair and put his head in his hands.

"What's wrong?"

"He was Jewish. He came here from Germany three years ago. I convinced the town to hire him for the school, and helped him set up a false identity."

"Dear Lord!"

"Exactly. I don't know how they picked him out."

We worked in silence for hours. It wasn't until we returned home that I showed him the document the soldiers had left behind. Father looked at it for a moment, then crumpled it and lit it on fire with his cigarette before he threw it into the empty fireplace. When I asked him why, he said he would never take Nazi money.

I stayed in the village for two more years. I saw many more Nazi convoys come through the village. Father and I built a false wall in the back of the store and kept half our stock hidden, as every convoy would empty our shelves and leave another voucher in payment. We lost money, but our neighbors made sure we did not go hungry.

Life moved slowly, and we heard very little about the war going on far beyond our borders. An occasional newspaper, left at the train depot, would make the rounds through the village. The outside world stayed outside.

16

By the spring of 1942, I thought I had chosen the direction of my life. I worked in the shop, although few people had money for much. A doe-eyed young woman spent more time picking through her order than was necessary, and she always had a smile for me. I tried to find what pleasure I could in life. It was not a peaceful time, but we endured.

I had just finished hiding a crate of salted pork behind the false wall, and was bent over, brushing the dust off my knees, when I spotted a very shiny pair of shoes. I looked up into the face of Vavrinec. I let out a laugh and grabbed him in a hug.

"What are you doing here?"

He returned my embrace, but when he let me step back, his face did not have the normal joy I was used to.

"What is it?"

"Jan…It's Father Josef."

My heart skipped several beats.

"What about Father Josef?"

Vavrinec picked up a jar of beets from the shelf and stared at the label I'd glued to it. He set it down and moved several of the things on the shelf around.

"Vavrinec, you're scaring me. What's going on?"

He gave a great sigh and looked at his shoes.

"He's dead. Father Josef is dead."

I don't know how I ended up sitting on the floor. I was just there, trying to breathe, blind from the tears. Vavrinec sat down next to me. He knew how much that old man meant to me. He'd visited me often at the warehouse church, just to pass the time, and he and Father Josef had known and liked each other. More than once, Father Josef said Vavrinec was good for me, to keep me from too much seriousness.

When I could breathe again, I asked the question I wasn't sure I wanted an answer to, my eyes focused on a knot in the wood floor.

"How did it happen?"

"He was shot. I don't know why. After you left, I visited him pretty often, to see if I could help with anything."

"Help?"

"I've been making some…business arrangements that aren't exactly allowed by the government."

"Black market?"

He didn't answer, but moved on to his story.

"I went to see him last week. He wasn't in the church, so I went up to the apartment. I checked his office, but he wasn't there either. When I knocked on the apartment door, it came open. Someone had torn the rooms apart. I found…"

His voice choked off. He coughed and tried again, with a sob in his words.

"I found Father Josef in the kitchen. He'd been shot."

"Mother, have mercy!"

"I went to the Cathedral and forced my way into the Bishop's office. He couldn't come with me, but he sent some men. We waited until it was dark and snuck Josef's body out in a car. We buried him that night. I guess the men were priests."

I sat without speaking for a very long time; long enough for Vavrinec to get up to close and lock the front door; long enough for the sun to slant through the windows; long enough for Father to come looking for me. When he arrived, I told him what Vavrinec told me. He didn't say much; instead, he led us both home.

At home, Mother and Ryba cried over the news; they all knew Father Josef from my stories. I tried to eat, but my stomach hurt too much, and I left the table early. Vavrinec found me outside, looking up at the stars.

"I didn't just come to tell you about Father Josef, Jan. Before I left, I told the Bishop what I intended to do, telling you, and he gave me this."

He handed me an envelope and went back inside. I recognized the Bishop's seal on the flap. I went back to my room before I opened the envelope and read the letter by candlelight.

Dear Jan,

By now, your friend has explained what happened. I share your grief; Josef was a good friend. He was one of my teachers when I was younger than you, and I feel lucky to have known him.

I know we have not done well where you are concerned. Two years is too long, and I would expect you to move on with your life. But if you still want to be a priest, I have an offer for you: if you return to Brno, I will ordain you.

I have a need for you, but I cannot write about it here.

Whatever your decision, you have my blessing.

Kupka

I prayed that night for Father Josef, and for the wisdom to know what to do. I had worked so hard, for so many years, to become a priest. I entered the Seminary when I was barely sixteen, and until the day I left, the priesthood was the central focus of my every action. And here it was, within my grasp. I could reach my goal, and fulfill the potential Father Josef saw in me.

But I had spent the last two years building a new life. I was proud of the work I had done in Father's store, of the help I'd given the people of my village. Because of me, few of our neighbors went hungry, even when the Nazis raided my shelves. Because of my work, we survived easily through the winter. Because I stood between the Nazis and the villagers, nobody else had put himself close to Evil. My village, my home were better because of me.

I thought all night, staring at the ceiling of my childhood bedroom. When dawn cracked through my window, and I could smell Father's morning tea, I was no closer to a decision than when I went to bed.

When I came into the kitchen, Vavrinec was entertaining Mother with an impersonation of me trying to dance the first night he met me. As I stood in the doorway, everyone stopped moving as they spotted me, then burst into laughter. I smiled with them, but did not say anything at first. Instead, I showed the letter to my parents. When he had read it, Father stood up from the table and started toward the door. I called after him.

"Where are you going?"

He turned in the doorway and gave me a smile.

"You'll need a ticket to get back to Brno."

17

I took the stairs of the warehouse church as slow as I could. I wanted to see where Father Josef died, but I feared the memories and ghosts that waited.

When I had left, my office had been clean and orderly, mostly from a lack of use. I met most people on the street or in the church itself. But when I looked in, the desk was overturned against a wall, the drawers scattered around the room. I found the fountain pen my father gave me when I entered Seminary; I had forgotten it when I packed. I slid it in my pocket, then gave the room a longer look.

The office had been very small. But it seemed smaller than I remembered. I picked up the chair and looked at the window in the back of the room. That window had been directly behind the desk, and gave me some light in the middle of the day. But the window was against the wall, and the desk couldn't have been centered on the window itself.

I turned in the chair and looked at the door. It sat flush against the wall, perpendicular to the doorway. The handle had sometime hit the wall hard enough to break through the plaster. I remembered the mark, but I thought the door opened further.

It hit me; the wall came about a meter closer to the door than it had. The old door mark had been against the same wall as the doorway, and the door used to open fully. The window had been in the middle of a wider wall. The room was smaller.

I closed the door and poked my finger into the hole caused by the door handle. My finger went through the plaster, and several chunks came away. I looked through and saw daylight.

I left the office and went into the apartment. My old bedroom shared a wall with my office. I started through the door, but stopped. My office was torn apart; my room had been destroyed. The wall shared with my office had been savagely ripped out, and chunks of plaster and lathe covered the floor. I couldn't tell if the room was smaller or not because of the debris.

I picked my way across, doing my best to avoid nails. The new space had not been large; inside, three chairs sat in a row. A flash of color caught my eye, half covered by plaster dust: a doll. I brushed off the dust and looked at it. It was crude, but the painted on face smiled at me. The dress showed wear from a child's arm.

I carried the doll through the apartment. Josef's room looked disturbed, papers thrown around, but nothing destroyed. In one corner, I found his emergency kit: a leather satchel with stole, pyx, oil, and breviary. He kept it with him at all times, slung over his shoulder. Even in class, he kept it close at hand. I could not leave it on the floor.

With the doll in one hand and the satchel in the other, I searched through the rest of the apartment. In the kitchen, a large, black stain discolored the floor. I knelt down and ran my fingers over the stain, my breath hesitant as I made contact.

When I stood, a great anger came over me. I shouted my rage and slammed my fist against the kitchen counter. I heard a thump as something heavy fell onto the shelf below. I stooped over and reached into the dark cupboard. Cool metal met my hand, and when I pulled it out, I held a heavy, dark revolver.

Father Josef died right next to this counter. He must have been trying to get the gun, to defend against whoever came in. I weighed the gun in my hand for a moment, then tucked it into my belt, hidden under my jacket. I did not know what I intended to do with the gun. When I left, I closed the door behind me; Josef would not want me to leave it hanging open.

I stopped in the church, but the dust was several weeks thick; the parish would not return.

I rode my motorcycle slowly through the city. Soldiers stood at every main intersection, and stopped me twice to examine my identification papers. None of them bothered to search my saddlebags, where I had placed the satchel and doll.

To reach the Cathedral, I had to cross the railroad. As I pulled up, a train came through, blocking me. I did not pay it much attention, as it started past, until something in one of the slow-moving cars caught my eye: through the high window, I saw several hands, reaching out to grab at nothing.

I looked closer; these were not meant to carry people. As a boy, I'd seen sheep herded onto these cars, but never people. Yet, as I watched, hands and faces became visible, peeking through gaps in the slats.

On the caboose, a pair of German soldiers smoked as they leaned on the rail, talking, their rifles casually hung from their shoulders. They ignored me as they went past.

I sat on my motorcycle in disbelief; they were hauling humans like livestock; car after car, full enough that every window was packed with faces.

The train was long past when I finally started my motorcycle and drove the rest of the way to the Cathedral. Back home, we knew little about what happened beyond the village streets and farms. The anger I felt in the apartment came back. I wanted answers.

18

I burst through Bishop Kupka's office door with neither invitation nor grace, but when he saw me he lost the instinctive anger that sprang to his face.

"Jan! We expected you a few days ago."

"I've been staying with a friend. What is going on? What happened at the church? Why did I find this in the apartment?"

I pulled the pistol from under my jacket and tossed it on his desk. He flinched at the thump.

"Be careful with that!"

I opened my other hand and showed him the bullets; I'd unloaded it before I entered the Cathedral.

"Why did Josef have this?"

"Please, sit down. I can answer some of your questions."

"Start with the gun."

Bishop Kupka sighed and slumped in his chair. He put his hand over his eyes, and murmured, almost too quiet for me to hear.

"I told him not to keep that."

"Bishop, I…"

"He had the gun because he was hiding Jews. You saw the wall, right? A family came to him and asked him for help. He built that hiding space and kept them in the apartment. I don't know how the Germans found out, but they did."

"Is that when they shot Josef? When they came for the family?"

"I assume so. I don't know for sure. Where did you find the gun?"

"Hidden in the kitchen."

"Next to where he died."

I nodded.

"Did you find anything else?"

"A doll."

I showed everything I found; he picked up the doll and ran his fingers over its face.

"I met the family when I visited Josef. The girl was about eight, I think. She had such a pretty smile. The whole time I was there, she held this in her lap. Her mother told me she never went anywhere without her dolly."

"What happened to them?"

He wiped his eyes and blew his nose before he answered.

"As far as I know, they were put on a train for Poland. That's what's been happening: the Nazis round up any Jews they find and put them on trains for Poland."

"I saw one of those trains, today. What are they doing with them in Poland?"

"I don't know. The official "news" says they are being moved for their own safety, but nobody believes it."

I got up from the seat and walked around the room. I ran my fingers over the picture frames along the walls.

"Are you doing anything?"

"Such as?"

"Such as anything to help."

"There is little I can do, Jan. I've tried writing to Rome, but I have no way of even knowing if my letters arrived. I've received no reply. And I cannot easily leave the Cathedral. The few times I've left, it's been in disguise."

In frustration, I grabbed a ceramic bowl from a shelf and started to throw it. As my arm moved back, I stopped myself.

Smashing the bowl would do nothing; I needed to be useful, not destructive. I put the bowl back and turned back to Bishop Kupka.

"Why did you ask me to come back?"

"Because of Josef. Because it is what he would have wanted. Because I have a use for you."

"A use?"

"Do you still want to be a priest?"

I thought for a moment. Much of my anger was toward the Church's inaction. Did I really want to join something I came close to hating? Then I thought of Josef. He saw enough real Good in the Church to dedicate his life to it. I nodded my head.

"Don't answer so quickly, Jan. If you agree to what I have in mind, you will not be a regular priest. I need someone who can move through the population without being noticed, someone invisible. The Nazis aren't very friendly towards the Church right now, and they watch all the known priests very close. Josef was not the first I've lost. In the last year, 8 of my priests have just disappeared. I have no idea if they are alive."

"But you think it has something to do with the Nazis." It was not a question.

"Everything has to do with the Nazis anymore. My priests cannot reach the people who need them anymore. That is not acceptable."

"How do I fit into all this?"

"As far as the Nazis are concerned, you're a former student who left Seminary without finishing. That is as far as your formal paperwork goes. You would be expected to attend Mass, but what you do with the rest of your time would be beneath notice. You can be invisible."

"How would I be a priest?"

"By doing all the things my priests cannot do; visit the sick, bless the dying, bring Christ to those who need Him. And, since you will be moving around, you can keep an eye on what is going on in the city and around the country. The Church is not officially doing anything. But, someday, all this will be over, and I refuse to let the evils done be forgotten by history. There will be a time of earthly reckoning."

The fierceness in his eyes frightened me; I did not want to be on the receiving end of this man's anger.

"So, I'll ask again. Do you want to be a priest?"

I thought about Josef, protecting a family at the risk of his own life. He taught me more about being a priest in the time I spent in the warehouse church than I learned in Seminary. I looked at the little doll, still on Kupka's desk. I almost believed I saw sadness in its eyes.

"When do I start?"

19

Bishop Kupka told me to make a presence in the city. I stayed with Vavrinec for several days before moving into a tiny apartment near the train station. Bishop Kupka found a parishioner near me who let me hide my motorcycle in his garden shed. I walked through the city for hours every day, watching the people, watching the soldiers, watching everything. I kept a notebook with me at all times, and made up a code to help me remember details, but which looked like gibberish to anyone else.

While I waited, I also visited the Cathedral every morning for daily Mass. I sat in the back, and stayed after the service, praying while the other people filed out. When I was alone, I would make my way to the Bishop's office, and he would go over the details I needed to know for ordination.

One morning, while we met, one of the Cathedral priests burst into the office.

"Your Excellency! The Nazis!"

"Calm yourself, father. What about the Nazis?"

"The Germans. Father Anton told us. Someone tried to kill Heydrich. All the soldiers are out there murdering people!"

I was confused.

"Who is Hedrich?"

Kupka turned to me and spoke in an offhand way.

"He's the man Hitler sent to be in charge of Czechoslovakia. He's a murderer."

"And someone tried to kill him?"

"Apparently so." He turned back to the priest. "Do you know what happened?"

"No, Excellency. Father Anton just ran in and told us about Heydrich. I think he has a radio. And, when I looked out the window, I saw a large group of soldiers come down the street."

"I see. Thank you, Father. Go round up the others. Tell them to be ready to help anyone who comes here. If the Germans come in, give them anything they want. Jan, you come with me."

He strode out of the room and I had to jog to keep up with him. He gave me instructions as we went.

"You need to get out of here, Jan. If the Germans do come in, and I expect they will, I don't want them to find you; that would ruin the whole plan. Do you think you can make it back to your apartment?"

"I think so."

"Go there; stay safe. I'm going to go out and see if I can help."

"I'd rather go with you, sir."

"I know you would, son. But I need you to be safe."

I knew he was right. But I didn't have to like it. Reluctantly, I left the Cathedral and started down the hill.

I only made it a few blocks when I met the Germans. They did not parade down the streets in rigid ranks; they were armed Rage in uniforms. They carried their rifles in their hands and aimed at anyone who didn't get out of the way quickly enough. I ducked into the first shop I could, a jewelry store. The owner started at my sudden intrusion, but only for a moment.

I started to tell them what was going on in the street, but the door was kicked open before I could get very far. Three German soldiers came in and pointed their guns at the owner. One shoved me to the side and told me to stand there and keep my mouth shut. I didn't dare disobey. They said they were searching for rebels.

I tried not to show my panic. I knew the only "rebel" in the building: me. The one nearest the door turned the lock and closed the curtains over the windows, leaving us in a premature twilight. He stayed by the door and kept an eye on me. The other two kept yelling at the owner, *where are the rebels, where are the rebels*, until he wept with fear and huddled on the floor. One of them suddenly grinned at the other one.

"I bet I know where they are. They're in here." He pointed at the displays of watches and rings in the glass counters. The other agreed, and they smashed the butts of their rifles through the glass.

It only took them a few moments to fill their pockets and satchels with the jewelry. When they finished, they turned back up to the owner, to threaten him some more I imagine. But they didn't say anything. They just looked at him for a moment, then walked back to the door where the remaining soldiers stood. The last one to leave looked at me and gave me a wink. To them, I became part of the crime.

The owner curled on the floor, protective, as if he held a great treasure in the fists clenched at his stomach. But he did not breathe anymore. Fear killed him as easily as a bullet.

I said a prayer over him; the poor man had done nothing, had not even protected himself. I did not want to leave him, but I could not stay. Bishop Kupka wanted me to stay safe, but I could not hide while this horror continued.

Outside, most of the soldiers had moved on from the street, and people were coming back out. I joined the people as we looked at the damage. Some with small wounds wore homemade bandages. I heard someone call my name.

Bishop Kupka had spotted me from across the street as I came out of the shop. He was dressed in a secular suit and carried a briefcase, and was going from shop to shop, checking inside each.

"Jan? What are you doing here?"

"I couldn't get through. Please don't sent me away; I need to help."

He looked at me for a moment, then nodded.

"Alright. I can use you. But keep your hat pulled down. Don't forget, you have a larger job to do later."

We entered the shop and I showed Kupka the dead man. He knelt at the man's side for a moment before he opened his briefcase and pulled out a vial of Holy Oil and a short purple stole. He gave the blessings and prayed over the body while I kept watch at the door, a mirror to the soldiers. The rite took only a few moments, and when he joined me at the door, he still had his stole around his neck.

"There will be more. We must see to them."

He did not speak to me for the rest of the afternoon. We went from door to door, following, as best we could, the route the Nazis had taken earlier. We went from chandler to bakery, from dressmaker to silversmith, from apartments to cafes. Sometimes we found the bodies. Sometimes their families found us. Twice I had to run back to the Cathedral for supplies of Holy Oil.

Others joined the work. At the Parnas Fountain, we found three Orthodox priests attending to a crowd of schoolchildren. None of the children were injured, but the priests were keeping them together while others of their order went to their homes to bring their parents and to check for any horrors that would await the children. We were needed elsewhere, so left them as they sang happy songs to keep the children calm.

Night fell before we made it home. We stopped twice on the way for patrols of soldiers under orders to enforce a curfew. It was only the commandant's Catholicism that saved us from arrest. Others did not fare so well.

The funerals took more than a week.

20

I let a week pass after the last funeral before I returned to the Cathedral. Bishop Kupka told me to stay away, in case the Germans kept a closer watch after their destructive actions. When I found him in his office, he had his back to the door, looking out his window. He didn't turn around when I entered.

"From up here, it's all so beautiful still. I cannot see the ugliness until I come down."

He turned to me.

"We cannot delay any longer, Jan. Are you ready?"

"Yes, Excellency."

"Then follow me."

He led me through the maze of the Cathedral basements to a little room, far from all the public areas. Even by candlelight, the dust on the floor showed several recent shoeprints.

"This was once the Bishop's private chapel, long before I took my first steps toward priesthood. My predecessor used this room as a wine cellar, but I believe we can use it for it's original purpose."

He pulled open the door and showed me the room. Cut into the rock of the hill, the room barely had space for three men to stand. A narrow Prie Dieu stood in the center of the room, and a tiny table made do as an altar. Bishop Kupka went through the room and lit several candles, creating a dance of shadow and light.

"Kneel and pray, Jan. I need one more thing and we can begin."

I knelt and bowed my head. This was far from how I imagined my ordination would be. Upstairs, in the main body of the Cathedral, generations of Seminarians had knelt before the huge altar, surrounded by the golden walls, as friends and family filled the pews. The line of priests would stretch across the entire front of the church in welcome. The air rang with songs of joy.

But not for me; I knelt underground, alone. My family was far away, and the priest who would have been my sponsor was dead. I prayed for all of them, and for guidance.

I heard footsteps outside and the door opened to reveal Bishop Kupka and another priest, who carried a large, red leather covered book. I recognized him as the Bishop's personal secretary, a bookish and exacting man named Father Anton. I rose and bowed my head to them. Kupka opened the book and set it on Father Anton's arms as a makeshift lectern.

"We're ready to begin."

Bishop Kupka proceeded to question me on Church doctrine. Our evening conversations came back to me, and I gave the answers. When I finished, the Bishop stood next to me and faced the altar. He spoke in the formal tone he reserved for Mass.

"We rely on the help of the Lord God and our Savior Jesus Christ, and we choose this man, our brother, for priesthood."

Then he turned to face me and grasped my hands.

"Do you swear, before this witness, to serve Christ and our Holy Church, and to obey the instructions of your superiors?"

"I do."

In the tiny room, I prostrated myself, my feet against the back wall, my head shy of the altar by the width of a book. Bishop Kupka and Father Anton started the Litany of the Saints, one of the main prayers I studied from my first days here. Father Josef had helped me remember the responses needed. While I lay on that cold, stone floor, I could hear his growl as he prompted me.

I thought of Father Josef and all he had taught me. In another world, he would bless me and drape the alb and stole around my neck. He would sit at the table during the celebratory dinner, next to my family, and tell stories of my days in the Seminary. When I grew scared of the future, he would answer my letters with his gruff affection and the advice of his years.

Instead, he died, trying to defend a family. My hands clenched into fists. I came to Brno to become a priest; I lived every day since the first to reach this goal, and I could not share it with anyone I loved. Before the eyes of God, before the Bishop, before the Church, before the enemy in our land, I lay alone on a cold, damp stone floor.

As the prayers ended, I rose to my knees before Bishop Kupka. Both he and Father Anton placed their hands on my head and blessed me, and I prayed I would grow worthy of their faith in me.

The Bishop motioned for me to rise to my feet. Father Anton brought forward a small square of cloth. It received a brief blessing, then the two of them unfolded it: a stole. Not the long, lush silk I saw on priests as a child. The length of one of my arms, this color stole, violet, was worn by priests for Advent, Lent, and Last Rites. I looked at the Bishop.

"You are now a priest, but you will not be known. Your flock will be whoever is in need. Your church will be the open field, the barn, the cottage. We are at war. You are now our warrior. So many of our people are hurting, and we are few. We will be fewer. We are in the time of sacrifice, of fasting. The calendar does not matter now. We are in Lent, awaiting the Resurrection, the dawn.

"I should not ask what I must of you, my son. I do not fool myself to think we can save the lives of everyone. But we must try to save their hearts and their souls. Our people are calling out for God, and they cannot hear Him. We must let them know, God is still with them, even during this darkest evil."

I did not speak; I felt a twinge of embarrassment and guilt, thinking about the ordination I could not have, up in the Cathedral. I saw my worries as small, petty, when compared to the pain of my country. My fellow priests died for their beliefs; I could not let my wishes dishonor their sacrifices.

Bishop Kupka finished the Mass. The two men embraced me as their brother, then the Bishop and I moved to his office. Father Anton stayed behind to reorganize the chapel.

On his desk was a leather satchel; the one I had brought back from the warehouse church. Father Josef's kit. We did not sit, but stood facing each other as he opened the satchel and placed the items it contained, pyx, oil, and breviary, on the desk.

"I think he would have given this to you today, if he could."

He handed it to me.

I knew Father Josef was with me. I opened the book and found several pressed flower petals, roses from the Seminary garden. Josef, more than any of us, loved those roses.

I packed everything back into my satchel. When I looked up, Bishop Kupka held out a glass of amber liquor.

"I'm sorry we cannot do this the right way."

"I understand. This is right. I felt so useless when we tried to help the people in town. Now, I feel like I can do something for them."

"Today you gained earthly confirmation. But God chose you long ago to walk this path. We are just catching up to Him."

We drank as equals.

21

For the first while, Bishop Kupka kept me in Brno. I moved from church to church, carrying notes from the Bishop to the priests, and helping set up a network of messengers from among the young men and women of the parishes. I did not do anything I considered 'priestly,' but I did feel I helped.

During that time, the entire country lived in fear: Heydrich had succumbed to his wounds, and the propaganda sheets were full of entreaties and threats, looking for information. People disappeared.

One morning, Bishop Kupka met me in the back of the Cathedral after Mass.

"I received a message from some Polish friends, saying the Nazis are building up their stores near the border to use against the Soviets. If we can find where those depots are, my friends can destroy them and leave the Germans hungry. You can slip in on that motorcycle of yours, talk to the local priests, and be back here before anyone notices. Then I can get the information out."

I rode far to the north, further than I had ever traveled. I did not try to follow a route; I simply followed Bishop Kupka's instructions to see what I could see.

I avoided Prague, but the closer I came, the more soldiers I saw. I tried to avoid patrols as best I could; I used cattle trails and spent much time behind trees, holding my breath.

I did not know a town lay beyond the trees; I only turned toward it because of the birds. I was sure that many crows could not be good. When I heard the trucks, I drove into the forest to hide, but crept back to where I could see the road.

I did not count the number of trucks that drove past me, but they seemed to go on forever, each with a bed full of soldiers. The trucks drove slowly past me, and I could see dark splatters on the uniforms of several of the men. I thought they had been in a battle of some sort, but there were no wounded. No ambulance followed the trucks, and there did not seem to be any empty seat; just soldiers, holding their rifles.

I waited a short time after they passed before moving. I came back to the road and headed in the direction the troops came from. Before I traveled a kilometer, I found the town. A charred sign gave the name: Lidice. It held nothing. No people. No animals. Nothing but open doors and fresh tire tracks. Even the birds I first saw circled outside the village. I rode toward them until I found a place to hide my motorcycle, then walked the rest of the way. My stomach clenched as I neared a stench so foul I could see it like heat waves, radiating above the road.

Bodies. I did not know it was just men right away. Men and boys. But that is whom I was with: the men of the village, all dead in the farmyard, stacked on the bodies of their neighbors, their hands unbound, eyes open and staring.

I knelt at the first one I came to and pulled out my kit. By the time I knelt with the tenth man, I ran out of oil. By the twentieth, my thumb blessed them with the blood of their neighbors, picked up from the ones shot in the head. I did not mean to do it; I did not even noticed until I looked behind me and saw rows of men with bloody crosses on their foreheads.

I moved to the next man. I started the prayers and put my thumb to his forehead. His eyes opened and he made a terrible, soft croaking sound. I jumped back, my heart nearly frozen. I could see him struggle to breathe. His legs were under several other men. I tried to pull him out of the pile, but the weight trapped him. I pulled harder until I saw pain. I let him gently down and looked into his face.

"It will be alright. I've got you. I'm going to get you out of here."

He grabbed my wrist and held on.

"I won't leave you. I have to move these..." I couldn't say bodies. "I have to move them off of you."

He let go. I pushed the top man off his legs. He...it...rolled over. I tried not to look at the horrible wound in his chest. The next man weighed much more, and I could barely shift him. The living man moaned and I moved back to his head.

"Water."

I had left my canteen with the motorcycle, but I kept a small flask of holy water in my jacket pocket. I hesitated, but decided it could not be sacrilege. I held the flask to his lips and he sipped a few drops before he let his head flop back. He labored to breathe. I moved back to the pile of men and put my shoulder to the weighty one. He slid off. I went back to the living man's shoulders and pulled again. He came free, but a wound in his groin spurted blood. The men on top of him had cut off the blood flow. Without them, he bled. I put my hand to the wound, but I could not stop all the blood. I grabbed at the bullet-shredded shirt of one of the other men and ripped it from his body to use as a bandage. It soaked through in seconds.

"Please." His eyes stared at the blood on his leg. "Please."

I reached for his hand. He crushed my fingers with his grip.

I did not hear the truck engines, but I did hear when one blew its horn. I looked over to the road. I did not see anything, but I could suddenly hear the rumble. The Nazis had returned. I looked at the man who clutched me. I promised to save him, to stay with him. He had closed his eyes. His chest barely moved. I knew he would die very soon. I could not save him.

To save myself, I ran. I broke my promise to the man. I ran to the trees and hid.

I watched as the Nazis searched the bodies. The search through so many pockets would take hours. Everything found went into a sack guarded by one of the soldiers against his fellows. They did not trust themselves.

There was not much for the sack; fingers and wrists were checked and pockets rummaged, but with little result. The villagers owned no riches.

They searched the area where I left the man. The soldier, so young, jumped when he saw the man still lived. He called over to the nearest officer, who did not hesitate to step on the bodies as he walked to the soldier. He studied the man for a moment, then, without a word, drew his pistol and fired into the man's head. He patted the soldier on the shoulder before he returned to his inspections.

When they were done, they all tied cloths around their faces. The soldiers piled the corpses, an easy job since the bodies fell so close together. When they finished, five of them put canisters on their backs. Tubes rode around their shoulders to some sort of nozzle in their hands. They stood around the pile of bodies and pointed the nozzles at the pile of bodies. Fire erupted, and I wanted to close my eyes.

I could not leave. I wanted to, but I made myself bear witness. I could do nothing else for these men.

The burning took less than an hour. I tried to ignore the greasy, pork smell. The soldiers left the farm, but I could hear the sounds of destruction from the village for hours. Before dark, more clouds of smoke came from the soldiers' work as they tore down and burned every building.

I spent the night in that grove of trees. At first light, I pushed my motorcycle under a thick bush and walked south; afraid I would be arrested if I rode away from the village. I stopped to wash at a little stream. The water turned dark where I scrubbed my hands and face; I was wearing the ashes.

My stomach turned at the memory of what I had seen. More, I felt sickened by my own cowardice. I hid to protect myself, instead of performing the duty ordained to me a scant few weeks before. I had failed my first test.

I could not face Bishop Kupka. He trusted me to do the right thing, and I had failed him. He chose me from among my fellows to go out into the world and help, and I hid in the face of my own danger.

I looked at my face in the water as the ashes from my hands drifted away. I decided to do the same, to drift away like ashes in a river. I could not return to where I came from, so I would find a new

place to be.

Part 2:

Priest

1

A priest without a church is unframed. The physical church is

not just a building; it's a home. The Fathers speak of "the House of

the Lord," but it is so much more than just a house. A priest is judge

and doctor, teacher and lawyer, advocate and defender in the eyes of

a community, and the church is the first and last place the faithful

go. In times of great joy, the priest blesses the bounty of the

community. In times of sadness, the priest offers comfort and

healing. In times of peril, the church and priest offer sanctuary in a

tradition inviolate by all but the cruelest. The church is the home to

the heart of the faithful community, and without a church and a

priest, the community is lessened.

These were the thoughts I did not have as I ran from the

horror of Lidice.

I had never been a hiker or hunter. Father forbad guns in the

house, a leftover of his time during the Great War. My play was in town and ended when Mother called me in for dinner. The woods, the wilds, the open spaces were not my place.

I didn't fear the daylight. But night under a tree, too scared to light a fire and no means to light one anyway, I could not remove the images I had seen. When I did sleep, my dreams were filled with piles of dead men, their arms stretched toward me. Wind through leaves sounded to my ears like the hiss before ignition of the flame-thrower. During the day, they just sound like leaves. During the day, everything is what it is.

The rest of the world fought each other, with bombs and guns, ships and airplanes. Our country never had the chance to fight; our army was stopped before it could even start. In terms of the war, Czechoslovakia sat deep behind the lines, removed even from our own name. Yet, every road and town was patrolled. In my mind, I knew I had no reason to hide from them; if I had been seen in Lidice, I would have been shot. In my mind, I was safe; in my heart, I knew I was in danger.

I walked South. I avoided cities and towns and traded labor for food and shelter at any farm that would have me.

I stopped to help an elderly couple. The husband, bent from a life behind the plow, leaned against the woodpile to oversee my work, his hands too gnarled to grip the axe. He directed and criticized my woodcutting abilities, and inspected every chunk as if flew off the stump, obviously inferior to what he would have done, were our roles reversed. From the house, his wife commented with laughter.

"Don't listen to him; he hasn't been happy for fifty years."

His growled response was something about a wedding, but I chose not to catch all of it.

After I finished the wood, the wife brought out three glasses of beer and, with a teasing smile towards her husband, gave me first choice of the glasses. I could not hide my smile; their bickering came with smiles and shared laughter.

The husband started to tell me about his married daughters, and how their husbands usually divided the farm labor, when we heard a noise from the road that set my heart racing: the deep growl of a large truck. My throat closed over when I spotted the green canvas of a military vehicle.

The truck came after a smaller vehicle, which led it from the road to the house. I wanted to run in panic, but I feared the soldiers would take their anger out on the couple, if I happened to escape.

None of us moved as the vehicles ground to a stop in front of the house. I leaned against the woodpile, next to where the axe sat. I did not touch it, but the soldiers could not allow me to be near a weapon. One of them pointed his gun at me while two others came forward. The smaller soldier grabbed the axe and tossed it into some deep weeds, while the other threw me to the ground and placed a foot on my back.

Fear is a flavor; it is thick and bitter, almonds left to rot. My stomach wanted to vomit, but fear closes a throat. The Nazis had occupied Czechoslovakia for five years, and I'd had several experiences around soldiers, but never had one pointed a gun so near my head. I heard the old man protesting that he had nothing to hide. The couple clung to each other; the years having shaped them into perfectly fitted pieces that supported their whole, no matter what; she tucked herself under his arm, seeking the protection he could no longer provide.

I could hear the house being dismantled from the inside. A home protects the fragile artifacts of life. These were poor people. What little they had was in the house; what little they had became shards. The soldiers' search took very little time in reality, but I could not see what was happening for an eon at least. I only looked up when I heard the engines fade into the distance.

The couple did not weep. They simply stood in their doorway and took stock of what remained. Their little house, built by their own hands from rough fieldstones, still stood. It looked as it had when I arrived, a loved and cared for home. I saw my satchel and walking stick were where I had left them on the ground next to the woodpile. I picked them up and went inside.

The old man stood next to the overturned table. I helped him try to right it, but one of the legs broke off as we got it level. The man's voice broke.

"I made this. Back before we married. She told me we would need a big table; she wanted many children. So I made this. It was so big, I had to take it apart to get it through the door."

He hung his head in shame and his wife led him to a chair and cradled his head to her bosom. I leaned the table back on its side and looked at the leg; it had snapped off completely. I could hear his wife comfort him.

"Shhh, darling. You can fix the table. It will be stronger than ever. Will you do that for me?"

He nodded against her.

"Of course."

On one wall hung a Crucifix, a roughly made cross of twisted and knotted wood, held together with tarnished wire. I pulled my stole and prayer book from my bag and knelt before the Cross. My movement caught the wife's attention and she joined me in prayer. The old man could not kneel, but he did sit with us. I could not think of any prayer for a destroyed home, so I prayed a thanksgiving for our survival.

When I was done, the wife asked if I would hold a Mass. Their old priest had been killed over a year ago, and the country church had been empty since. I was scared I would be discovered, but these people were so earnest I could not refuse them. We set off for the church on a path between ancient fields of new hay. Any neighbors we came across were sent off to gather their families to the church.

This was my first public Mass. At the Cathedral, my Priesthood had been a secret, and I simply had not had a chance before. The church was roughly built from time-bleached grey wood, but cleaner than any other building I had seen in the area. The wife explained how the women took turns to come each week and clean, because God should not live in a dirty house.

The vestments had been looted, but we were able to celebrate with what we had. One family brought enough bread to be shared, another a dusty bottle of wine. I blessed them all and preached to them the story of Job. When we were done, they all promised to keep me a secret.

That was the only time I revealed myself on my journey.

2

I kept my vocation a secret, though it pained me. In Brno, I could go to the Cathedral, and for a few hours could be my true self. In the wilderness, as I wandered, I kept my secret. The story of a wandering priest could bring the sort of attention I did not want. I took a very real chance when I prayed with the elderly couple and their neighbors, but they promised to protect me, and I believed them.

Life on the road was harder than I imagined. As a boy, I read stories of knights and heroes, going on adventures across the countryside. The stories never mentioned the dust and dirt, rain and mud, howling winds and throbbing sun. I knew other men could survive like this, but I had neither the skills nor the provisions to stay out in the wilderness for long. I needed a place, both for shelter and to let me pay my penance. I needed a place where I could help.

I picked my destination with care. Nikde is an anonymous sort of place. I traveled there once with Father. I remember the coal dust on the lintels of every business where the miners brushed their hands and clothes on their way through their daily realities. Every house we passed had a door in the front for visitors and one on the side with a wash bucket and a bar of yellow soap streaked with black.

I did not choose Nikde to be a miner. I have less business in a mine than I do in a forest at night. No, I chose it because I could not think of a place I would be needed more. Occupation made near-slaves of miners, as the Great Nazi Beast needed feeding far beyond what Germany could provide. Those underground had no choice but to collaborate with our enemies. Their families live in the town, and the Nazis had shown their willingness to exact revenge and reprisal.

Man is not meant to go into the earth, until death. But these men do, and come back as shades, pale beneath the darkness of their trade, when they come back. Death dances in a mine, and there is nothing doctors can do to fight him. Miners go into the darkness every day of their lives. I could not let them go into the next world alone.

The mine's hospital was temporary in the way only a fifty year old building can be. There were no rooms, no privacy, no place for those tough, strong men to give in to the human weaknesses of illness and pain without an audience. The canvas walls and roof were more stitches than whole, and the beds had their own roofs to keep the rain off their tenants.

There was no surgery ward. An injured man stayed in one place until he either walked out or was carried. The medical interventions from the minuscule staff were brutal and necessary. If something couldn't be mended, set, or stitched, it was removed.

I arrived long after the Nazis and brought with me nothing more than a willing set of hands. Dr. Golc, the only person in the mining camp with any medical training, interviewed me by having me help hold down a miner whose leg had been broken by a runaway cart. Four of us, three of the miner's friends and me, piled on top of his arms, chest, and unbroken leg. A fifth man folded his leather belt in half and shoved it between the patient's teeth, then held his head still. When we were all in position, Dr. Golc grabbed the man's foot and gave a hard tug. The man screamed into the belt as his bones ground against each other.

I suppose Dr. Golc was satisfied with the setting of the break. He told us to stay where we were while he splinted the leg and wrapped it in long bandages. When he had tied the last knot, we all stepped back from the man. He spat out the belt and gave each of us a description of the means by which our mothers and various animals had predicated our births. I believe mine had something to do with a fish.

The doctor picked up a large bottle from next to the bed and uncorked it. The patient's eyes lit up when he saw the bottle and he reached for it eagerly. The doctor let him drink from it, and then raised it to his own lips. He passed it to the man next to him, and the bottle circled until it came to me. I had no idea what I was holding, but I didn't want to stand out from the group. When the liquid hit my mouth, my tongue went completely numb and the small cracks in my lips from my long journey burst into flames. My best effort at manliness ended with me choking, the men laughing, and the doctor rescuing his precious bottle. The patient was given several more drinks until he nodded off and his friends left.

That was how I arrived at the Nikde coalmine hospital.

3

The Doctor and I were not alone in our work. One matron remained from before the Occupation. The only name she would respond to for the Doctor or myself was Mrs. Tasic, and any deviation would lead to a motherly evil eye.

Mrs. Tasic respected Dr. Golc's title, but had no respect for the man under the dingy white coat. As long as he was giving medical orders or opinions, she was a rapt audience. Any other time, he was just an annoying insect that best keep out of the way. The ward was her territory, and everyone remembered that.

I was not trusted with the sheets for the five cots, nor with the tiny pharmacy. I could, however, lift and move things as long as I was under strict supervision and didn't try to rearrange the placement from The Great Plan.

It was Mrs. Tasic who discovered my secret. One of her duties when there was someone in one of the cots was to check on them several times each night. My room was connected to the ward, so when one of the men started thrashing and coughing, I was on hand to assist her in restraining him. I asked if one of us should run for the doctor, but she told me he wouldn't be able to help ease the pain better than she could herself.

I had been praying Compline when the commotion started, and had slid my breviary, chrism, and stole into my pockets when I rushed out to help. Mrs. Tasic left me alone with the patient while she went to the pharmacy. With her out of sight, I slipped the stole around my neck and started the Anointing of the Sick. I offered Absolution to the man for his sins, and when I crossed myself I heard a quiet "amen" behind me. It was Mrs. Tasic who had her head bowed over her hands. A second later, she was in charge again. She administered the shot of morphine to the man. We each took a seat on either side of his cot and began the long, final vigil.

The man slipped away before dawn. Mrs. Tasic sent me to fetch some help to move him to the town. I couldn't leave until I spoke about what she had witnessed.

"Mrs. Tasic," I started, but she cut me off.

"I will let you know which ones need your help. The Doctor is an atheist, but I don't think he will interfere or report you."

"Don't you want to know why I'm hiding?"

"No."

I left without another word. Mrs. Tasic was true to her word. At night I would occasionally hear a soft tap, and when I emerged she would point me toward a patient. Every time, the patient's wounds would take him away soon after I administered the Rite. She would not trouble me with someone she expected to survive. If someone else was in the room, she would shield my actions from them. I memorized the Rite, and practiced until I could say it in just a few moments. I could not anoint them, nor could I wear my stole most of the time. But somehow it felt right, as if I were finally following the Bishop's orders for me to be a warrior.

Between the two of us, very few souls slipped away alone.

4

We lived in a time and place of war, but the wounds we treated had nothing to do with bullets or bombs. Miners came to us in two groups: the broken and the dying.

The broken were the ones who survived cave-ins, dropping ceilings, accidents, and fights. The Doctor would set the bones he could and amputate the ones he couldn't. Many men walked around without all the fingers and toes they'd been born with. At the first call of a problem, the Doctor and I would rush up to the mine and treat the men as the other miners drug them to the surface. Any man standing around was drafted to carry the worst cases to the hospital while we treated those we could.

We worked in the dirt and soot on men blackened by their task. Within my first week, I helped the Doctor with three fast amputations on men who were still awake. After the first one, when the bleeding stopped and sleep calmed the man, the Doctor took me aside.

"You're doing well, boy. But you need to learn control. These men need us to look and act strong."

"How do I do that?"

"When they're on my table, they are no longer men; they're a wound. A wound feels no pain; a wound isn't scared; a wound isn't worried about a family to support. A wound is something I can fix. When that's done, they become people again."

"I don't know if I can do that."

"It will come to you. But for now, do your best to swallow your puke and keep your eyes on me. If you can't do that, I have no use for you."

The dying were the ones we could not help. It was not a lack of desire to help, or a lack of medical knowledge on the part of the Doctor. It is the coal miner's fate to die coughing. These were not young men who came to us. These were the life-long workers, who had started as soon as they were strong enough. They were legacies, third or fourth generation miners who had seen their fathers go down into the deep dark.

They all knew what was coming for them. When they came into our ward, we did what we could to make the comfortable. We had a small supply of morphine, and Mrs. Tasic would decide when each man would receive his shot. By the time they came to us, they had very little time left. The Doctor would send one of the young

miners to town to bring back whatever family could come.

There was one man like this in the ward when I arrived. I did

not learn his real name; everyone, even his wife, called him Goat.

His wife sat by the head of his bed during the day and returned to

town at night. Over the few days he lasted, his shift came to see him

in twos and threes. Each man would have his chance to speak

privately. I saw more than a few unlabeled bottles passed around.

The Doctor either pretended not to see what the men were doing, or

joined them for a drink. When there is no doctoring to do, any bit of

comfort is allowed.

Goat was one of the first men I blessed in the ward. Mrs.

Tasic and Goat's wife had washed him when he came in, but his face

and hands were lined in black, giving him an uneven striped look.

He was bald and pale between the soot, and his beard was long

enough for his wife to grab, a favorite way of getting his attention

according to his stories. She ran through her rosary while he told

dirty jokes and coughed up blood.

On the night before he died, I sat next to his wife and tried to

talk to her.

"How long have you been married?"

She held out her left and hand showed me her ring. I looked closer and saw it was made from a piece of bent wire.

"He put this on my hand thirty-two years ago. Had no priest in town back then. Just stood in my Mother's house and said we were married. Couple years later, priest came and said the words over us. But the first time counted."

Her hands shook, and I wrapped mine around hers. They were dry and cold, and I wanted to weep over them. But I did what the Doctor said: I looked strong.

"My father was a miner; brothers, too. Lost three of them in one cave-in, long time ago. Goat, here, he was an orphan. Wandered into town, thought he was about sixteen or so. Put in a day's work. Liked to sing as he went down the shaft. Always liked to pick me up when he hugged me."

I looked at her face; she looked at the man in the bed. I could tell she didn't see the shrunken, twisted, pained figure. She saw the youth, the boy he'd been.

I stayed with her that night. We did not talk. I was starting to learn, silence can be as precious as words. Toward morning, Goat started to cough up blood, but he never woke up again. He thrashed in pain, and I held down his shoulders so he wouldn't fall off the bed. I could not soothe him, but when his wife ran her gnarled fingers along his face, he settled down. Moments later, he died with a slight smile on his face.

When it was over, and his wife allowed her husband's workmates to lead her back to the village, I helped Mrs. Tasic clean up the body. When we finished, we wrapped him in a sheet his wife brought with her. I picked up the body to place it in the cart for the trip down the mountain. It, he, Goat, weighed so little. When we brought him in, I could barely lift his legs to get him on the bed. Death released all the pain. I hoped Goat was singing and smiling, young again.

5

I could not let myself forget why I came to the mine. I was still a priest, and I had a flock, even if they did not know it. One of the duties of every priest, as explained to me by Father Josef, is to provide comfort and protection for his congregation. I provided what comfort I could in the hospital. I could not protect the miners from the dangers of the mine. But those were not the only dangers in this life.

There were few young miners at Nikde. When Germany invaded, many young men joined the Army to defend our land. My own military experience was a two-day farce, but other men did face the Germans. Those men had not come home. Back at the Cathedral, I heard rumors of Czech soldiers keeping up the fight, refusing to surrender. They hid in the hills and fought a running war against an overwhelming enemy. Other rumors came about a government and army-in-exile.

This meant two problems for the miners. They simply could not continue the output of ore they had before the war. Without replacements for the injured and killed men, work at the mine slowed. Since the main customer of the coal was the Nazi state, a low output brought unwanted attention. And when that attention came in the form of inspections, the lack of young men in the mine and town led to questions about where those men were.

When I arrived, the mine had no Nazi presence. Within a week, the road to the mine was guarded by three platoons of German soldiers. I listened to the soldiers talk about the war as they walked through the mine grounds; some spoke about Russia, others about Poland. One said something about needing to keep the fires burning, to the amusement of his friends. I did not understand.

The only place in town that could be used for a barracks was an old chateau, but it was so full of unused mining, farming, and brewing equipment the commander decided to use the time-tested method of forced quartering of officers in the homes of citizens. The weather was still pleasant, so the soldiers simply camped in tents in the town square.

Every man in the mine was subjected to a twice-daily search, although what contraband they were looking for I could not imagine. I did not dare carry anything with me when I made the trip to town for supplies, and I made sure everything in the crates I brought back were supposed to be there.

My trips to town were infrequent. The Doctor usually had some of the miners bring the ordered supplies with them when they came on-shift. A few times, something was more important to him, and I was sent.

I cherished my time in town. The miner's mess was enough to keep body and soul together, but I was sworn to honesty and could not in good conscience call what they served "food." I was able to eat a real meal, drink a cup of coffee not brewed to the Doctor's horrendous taste, and read a newspaper. Even though the only one available was the Nazi propaganda sheet, it was still news of the world.

I returned later than usual one afternoon. I tried to time my arrival with the shift change, but this time the train had been late. I was the only person on the road to the mine, and the guard squad was able to give me their full attention.

"What is all this?"

"Just supplies for the hospital. Medicine."

The bottle of slivovitz the Doctor ordered garnered a very close inspection. The contents did not survive. They had just finished with me when a car pulled up to the barrier across the road. Every man but one snapped to instant attention. The lone holdout still held

the empty bottle as he urinated into the ditch. He was the youngest

man in the squad and the liquor had swayed his reason, as well as his

knees.

The car held the Commander in charge of the whole Nazi

contingent in Nikde, a one-armed combat veteran. He and his driver

exited the car and marched over to the squad. The Commander was a

gaunt man, nearly skeletal, and he played with a leather pouch on his

belt, just in front of his holster, whenever he spoke. He clicked it

open and shut, open and shut, so the sound of the snap acted as

punctuation for every statement.

"What have we here, gentlemen? A smuggler?"

"Sir, he claims to be the doctor's assistant at the mine

hospital."

"I see. And you don't believe him?"

"No, sir. We just had to be sure he wasn't a saboteur."

"A saboteur? Is his morphine supposed to explode? Maybe

he's making garrotes out of those sutures and plans to kill us all.

Gentlemen, have any of you seen him before?"

All of the men shouted the affirmative, except for the drunk one who was having an in-depth conversation with a tree.

"And has he ever brought anything but medical supplies through here?"

None of them spoke.

"I think, Feldwebel, we can safely assume this man is bringing a few supplies to the mine hospital. And I think you have something much more important to worry about than a box of medicine. You appear to have a drunk man in your squad."

"Yes, sir!"

"Where did he get the booze?"

The Feldwebel pointed at me. The officer turned to me.

"Were you trying to bribe my soldiers?"

"Bribe? No! We use this to dull patients' pain. We save the morphine for the worst cases since it's so hard to get. The slivovitz helps when we have to set bones."

"And how did the bottle come to be in the possession of my men?"

"I believe they were inspecting it to make sure it wasn't a bomb."

"I see. Feldwebel! You and your men are under arrest. You will return to camp and present yourself to the Officer of the Day. Have him send up a competent squad. I think that would be a pleasant change of pace. I will deal with your discipline problems when I return from the mine. Now, one of you raise that damn barricade before I decide the Fatherland would be better served by your executions."

He turned to me.

"I believe we can consider this matter closed."

"Yes, sir."

"Good." He stared at me for several moments, and then repeated himself.

"Good."

He turned quickly and stepped back into his car. The soldiers raised the barrier and the car went through. As soon as the car was out of sight, the squad grabbed the drunken soldier and dragged him down the hill. I packed up the remainder of my box and continued up the hill.

When I reached the hospital, a bottle of clear liquor sat next to the entrance.

6

To the men of the mine, we were a hospital. To the owners and the Nazis, we were in equipment repair. In either case, we were deemed important enough to avoid undo interference. After the incident with the guards, the hospital came to the attention of Rittmeister Ewald von und zu Kortig, the one-armed Commander of the local Nazi contingent. The soldiers saw Kortig's favor and acted accordingly.

Kortig had left his arm in Russia. During his one tour of the hospital, he spoke to the doctor about how our little setup was kin to the field hospital where his life was saved. He knew the conditions we worked under first hand and did what he could to ease our work. Any man we saved was one who could contribute to the German war effort, and that was Kortig's ultimate purpose.

Nikde was, for all intents and purposes, a fiefdom. Kortig was the lord of the realm for all matters military and civil. He was judge and jury for any suit or trial, and his punishments required public attendance for the people of the town.

Dr. Golc and I were exempt from this dictate. Mrs. Tasic, who lived in town on the few nights she was not on duty in the hospital, was not. She came with stories of executions and whippings, and that was just Kortig's own soldiers. The poor boy who got drunk from my bottle of slivovitz was hung from a tree for dereliction of duty and as an example to his men of the consequences to their actions, should they cross the line.

The civilian population did not come before him often. The fear of his judgments kept arguments from coming to official notice.

Crime does not end in a time of war. A young farm girl, certainly no older than fifteen, accused the son of a merchant of rape. He was one of the few young men still in the town, and was seen as the leader of the ne'er-do-wells of his generation. The girl's father was one of the poorest in the area, just above subsistence level. She would come into town for the few supplies the farm could not provide.

She accused the boy of dragging her into the alley behind his father's shop and holding a knife to her throat while he raped her. The boy's defense was that she had led him down the alley and seduced him. Her family screamed the outrage at this suggestion.

Kortig called for witnesses. All of the boy's friends swore the girl had seduced him with promises of her favor if he gave her a discount on her purchases. Nobody else in town could speak to the matter.

Except for me. I happened to have come for my own shopping that same day, and I heard the girl's screams for help. The boy had just fastened his pants when I arrived, and I saw him fold the knife and put it in his pocket as he walked away. I had covered the girl and helped her load her packages on her cart. I wanted to take her to see Dr. Golc, but she refused.

I stood before the court and told Kortig what I had seen. The only question he asked was if I knew either of the two young people before this incident. I did not, although I had met both of their fathers previously and knew them both to be good, honest men.

Kortig made us wait an hour while he decided what to do. The boy's friends spent the whole time staring at me and muttering threats of violence I could hear over the whispers of conversation around us. The girl's family spent the time bent over their Rosaries.

Kortig returned to the makeshift courtroom. The soldiers next to the boy pulled him to his feet.

"You are guilty. I say you are guilty, and, since my opinion is the only one that matters, this case is ended. You will be taken from this place to the village center, where you will hang from the neck until dead."

The boy's knees gave out and his guards had to hold him up as a puddle grew at his feet. The father of the girl stood and asked to be heard.

"Sir, I beg you to reconsider. The boy has done a heinous act on my daughter, but we do not wish death on anyone. Teach the boy. Punish the boy. But, please, do not kill the boy."

"You would ask this for the violator of your daughter?" Click, click, click: his fingers opened and closed the pouch on his belt with every word.

"He is still one of God's creatures, and we do not have the right to call for his death. This is what we believe."

Kortig did not show emotion. Instead, he turned to look at the boy.

"They ask for mercy. They are good people." Click.

He pulled out the pistol from his belt and held it against the boy's forehead.

"You are not a good person."

Everyone ducked when the gun sounded, and no one saw the boy fall to the floor. The screaming went on until the guards raised their rifles towards the crowd. Violence, so immediate, was a great reminder of our place in the world. Neighbors pulled the boy's mother away from his body and the room emptied until only I remained with Kortig.

"Do you not call this justice?" Click click click.

He was not asking me.

I could not speak. I could not look at him. After a moment, Kortig left the room. I was alone with the poor boy I had just sent to death. When I opened my mouth, vomitus sprayed down the front of my shirt.

I could not touch him to bless him. So I simply prayed. The guards removed the boy and mopped the floor. Only when there remained nothing but a damp spot on the floor could I move. I left and walked back to the hospital.

7

Where do we find forgiveness from the dead? Where do I? A boy lay dead because I told the truth of what I saw. Now the lives of his family are changed, broken, because I spoke the truth.

Is God even here? Have we been abandoned? Job went through trials for his love of God, while the pagans around him danced freely. We have all become Job, left to suffer because we are human.

Jews believe, to every generation is born a potential Messiah, to lead the world out of darkness. We believe he already came. But the darkness returned. Death. War. Famine. Pestilence. All exist now.

Maybe this is the final battle. Maybe this is the time when the Messiah returns, to call forth the souls of the righteous and end our known existence.

If he is to come, I hope he hurries.

8

The town was dying. The mine could not survive on the non-payments of the Nazis. Kortig and his men made sure they were the only customers, and within a few months there was no money for the miners. Commerce did not cease. Money was still necessary. But the miners could not buy anything from the shops in town.

No miners meant no patients for our hospital. Dr. Golc and I spent our time in Nikde, where there were still sick to see. Most were out of work miners, for whom time away from the dark wasn't a cure, just a delay. I was able to give blessings when the doctor would step out of the room to talk to the family.

One man was awake for my ministrations. When I started, he grasped my wrist with a strength he should not have had. His throat was raw from the cough. He should not have been able to speak at all.

"Priest?"

I nodded.

"Bless . . . Father . . . sinned . . ."

We continued as best he could. We finished before the others returned. The doctor and I stayed as he slipped away, but I noticed he breathed easier and his face was relaxed as he held his wife's hand.

I worried I would not be welcome in town after the trial. The family of the boy left soon after the funeral. They were not the only ones. Those who had somewhere to go and the permission to leave did. The rest stayed and tried to live as best they could.

A closed mine produces no coal, and the demand from the Nazis remained. We still lived in the hospital when the solution arrived.

The rail line in Nikde ran a spur up to the mine, to transport the ore away. In my time, the only cars to come to the mine were empty coal-haulers. We had not heard one for weeks, but were startled by the whistle one day in November. It pulled us from the hospital, where I was amusing myself by beating Dr. Golc at two-handed pinochle.

The train was different. Instead of the open-topped coal-haulers, passenger and boxcars were pulled up the hill. When the train stopped, Rittmeister Kortig stepped from the first car. He looked over the area, then yelled into the car for everyone to get to work.

Soldiers poured out, nearly twice as many as had been in the garrison. They fell into lines, then were set on tasks by their officers. Some started digging holes while others opened the boxcars and carried out wooden posts and bale after bale of wire.

Dr. Golc and I walked over to Kortig. He was on the edge of the activity, directing through aides and runners. He nodded to us as he finished a command to start two more latrine pits.

"Gentlemen. I am pleased to inform you that you are now in the employ of the Third Reich, locally under my command, through the generosity of the Fuhrer."

"What is going on?"

"We are reopening the mine. As the workers here are unwilling to contribute, I have made arrangements for other resources."

It took two months for the soldiers to set up the camp. The prison. We understood what the crude structures were as they took shape. If it were anything but a prison, the wire would have surrounded the entire compound. It did not.

Inside the fence, simple buildings were set up, hardly worth the name. Outside, a tent city gradually became a military camp.

Kortig and some of his officers took over the administrative building for themselves. And we . . .

We became a military hospital. Soldiers were assigned to us as corpsmen, although we had few patients, apart from a few construction accidents. Dr. Golc was given the honorary rank of Hauptmann, and I of Leutnant, so we might legally order the soldiers to their tasks. Mrs. Tasic did not receive a rank, but everyone, including Dr. Golc, continued to follow her orders without question.

9

It was Christmas Eve; my first as a priest. It was Christmas Eve when the first slaves arrived at the mine. That was not the name Kortig used for them. "Political Prisoners" had a much less menacing sound.

Uniforms are meant to remove all vestiges of individuality. The wearer is supposed to forget who they were before. The uniforms of the slaves made them invisible in the winter light. Grey men in grey stripes through the grey fog, against grey hills. Only numbers separated them from each other.

It was Christmas Eve; my first as a priest.

The grey men were herded from the train to the pens. They limped. Whether fatigue or injury, none were whole enough to merit the shouts and shoves of the guards. Like cattle, the grey men had to follow a fenced path, and each car unloaded only when the doors lined up. The first out were not living. The pile grew.

It was Christmas Eve; my first as a priest.

We had no snow yet. Only cold, only wind, only ice on the water in the tracks left by the military trucks as they brought what supplies had not come on the train. Only a hidden sky of no promise.

It was Christmas Eve; my first as a priest.

They would come in waves, eventually. The first grey men came to build barracks they would never occupy. More would go into the darkness. But this was their first day. They stood in lines, heads down, hands up when their number was called. No names. Never names. Humans have names. These were the grey men. These were shadows.

It was Christmas Eve.

I bore witness to their parade. The grey men did not move with hunger, or with anything else. I bore witness because to turn away would give victory to those who imprisoned them. I bore witness because, in spite of everything taken from them, they *were* humans, people, individuals, names, families. Those things do not disappear behind a row of numbers. They exist, hidden, stolen, broken. But they exist.

It was Christmas Eve. I celebrated my first Midnight Mass, alone but for Mrs. Tasic, kneeling before the tiny table that served as our Altar. Dr. Golc stayed in town with friends, and our hospital was empty. We prayed by the light of the candle Mrs. Tasic brought from home. We could hear the singing from the soldiers and the silence

from the prisoners.

It was Christmas Eve; my first as a priest.

10

The grey men came in waves as the camp grew. The first were the builders, who finished the barracks for the soldiers and added more structures to their own pen. They built tall watchtowers at every corner. They built a gallows next to the entrance of the pen. They built a second layer of fence outside the first, and the Germans filled the space between with broken glass.

These were not healthy men. They spoke the same Czech as the Jews who lived near my warehouse church. I did not recognize anyone; no man looks like his skeleton. They arrived weak, and working in the elements did nothing to strengthen them. Dr. Golc saw this immediately and grabbed his medical bag. We made it as far as the guard shack before a teenage junior officer stopped us.

"Sir, you are not allowed in this area. Military personnel only."

"Get out of my way, you idiot. I am going to examine those men."

"Sir, my orders are to stop anyone from entering the prisoner compound."

"Do your orders also say you are to allow an outbreak of disease? Do you think cholera cares about your pure, Aryan blood? Do you think germs will be stopped by a wire fence?"

The boy's hand moved towards his sidearm. He knew Dr. Golc outranked him, but he also had his orders from Kortig. He was very young.

"Son, take a look at those people behind you. Really look at them. Look at how much they are coughing. Maybe it is nothing. Maybe it is something that will spread through the whole camp and kill all of us. Do you want to be responsible for that?"

"No, sir."

"Then get out of my way. And open up that damn gate. I'm not going to crawl over the top of it."

We went into the compound, but I did see the young officer send one of his men up to the headquarters. A visit from Kortig was promised.

Two of the guards came in with us, with their rifles in their hands. They called the prisoners to line up outside the small building we commandeered for exams.

In my weeks in the hospital, I have seen men die. I have seen their bodies rebel against them. I have seen men weakened and weeping as they lose control over their own bowels. I have seen men crushed and limbless, coughing up blood and bile. I have seen many things.

But these men I had never seen. They stood; they walked; they breathed out of defiance for the harm done to them. Dr. Golc examined each man as he came in. Of them, ten were marked down as having communicable diseases that needed to be kept in check or they would spread.

It took the Doctor several tries before the men would give him their names. They had been trained to respond to the numbers on their arms and clothes only. After we had finished with the exams, we joined the guards outside and I called out the names of the men we wanted to take to the hospital. They would not come forward as the guards watched. It was not until I called the numbers I had jotted down next to their names that they stepped out of the lines. Dr. Golc was disgusted by my list, but he let me continue, since it was the only way to move the men.

I stood next to the men as we waited for Dr. Golc to finish. I tried not to let the foul smell that came from each man overwhelm me. I managed not to cough, but my eyes did water.

We told the guards we were taking the men to the hospital. The same young officer stood at the padlocked gate.

"Open this gate."

"Sir, prisoners are not allowed to leave the compound except for work."

"I am taking these men to the hospital before they infect the entire compound, you idiot."

Neither saw Kortig come up, but when he spoke the young officer turned pale and sprang to attention.

"What do you think you're doing, doctor?" Click click.

"I'm taking these men to the hospital. Two have pneumonia, one has what I suspect is tuberculosis, and the rest are showing signs of respiratory distress of some kind. I won't know what, exactly, until I can get them warm in the hospital."

"I see." Kortig stared over the heads of the prisoners. He put his hand to the pouch on his belt and clicked it open. Instead of closing it right away, he put his fingers in for several minutes before he spoke again.

"Which of these men are the worst, in your medical opinion."

Dr. Golc pointed out the three he had diagnosed and two others who were very weak.

"And you think they might spread disease if they stay in the camp?"

"I guarantee it."

"Well, we can't have that. Herr Leutnant! Take the five men Dr. Golc indicated and hang them. The rest may go to the hospital for examinations." Kortig pulled his hand out of the pouch and clicked it shut.

"Wait just a damn minute! These men are my patients, and I am not going to let you..."

I grabbed at Dr. Golc's arm, to keep him from attacking Kortig. It took all my strength to hold him back. Kortig would not hesitate to kill the Doctor, and I could not let that happen.

"Doctor, you have limited resources in both medicine and my tolerance. I am not going to allow you to waste time on men who are a danger to the rest of the camp." Click click click.

He gave the statue of the young officer a look.

"I gave you an order. Get to it. When you are done, burn the bodies. And cover your mouths with cloth while you do it. I don't want an outbreak in the barracks."

Click.

Dr. Golc stepped to the fence as Kortig turned away, but one of the soldiers aimed his rifle at him. The child-officer unlocked the gate and led his men inside, where the five men chosen for death were taken over to the ready gallows. The others were surrounded by guards and marched to the hospital. I started to follow, but saw the Doctor wasn't coming. He stood at the gate and watched as the nooses were tied.

The gallows stood so the condemned men faced out, towards the free side of the fence. Their eyes seemed to bore into me. God help me, I wished the Nazis had dropped hoods over their faces. I'd stood by as these men were taken from Dr. Golc; I did nothing. When the Nazi kicked the stool from under the first man, I closed my eyes. I heard the snap of the rope and the thrashing as the man twisted. I could not watch. As the second man dropped, I spun to my knees and vomited into the grass next to me.

Hanging is not a pretty death. The Doctor refused to look away.

"He took them from me. He took them from me." Over and over in a whisper as each living body dropped and twitched.

When the last was cut down, he turned and walked up the hill to the hospital.

We did not stay for the burning.

11

The five who survived the walk to the hospital did not heal. They had pneumonia, and no strength to combat it. The last died three days after we brought them in.

Dr. Golc insisted on conducting regular examinations of the prisoners. I would accompany him through the gate and keep watch while he treated patients with little more than a sharp knife and a bottle of aspirin. He lanced boils and treated fevers, but there was little he could do to cure starvation. A scrap of bread and a cup of tepid water with potato peels thrown in was not enough to keep men alive. And it didn't.

After the first time, we only brought one patient back to the hospital with us. Kortig had left for Prague and Dr. Golc bullied the guards into letting us take the old man from the compound. I tried to support the prisoner without looking like he needed it. Weakness was a death sentence.

We settled him in a bed, and he smiled as he sank into the unfluffable pillow as if it were stuffed from the king of ganders. Dr. Golc listened to his chest for several minutes, then closed his eyes and looked out the window. That told me louder than words that this was a terminal patient. He called Mrs. Tasic over and gave her the only instructions he could to make the man more comfortable: elevate his head and shoulders with pillows and boards and wrap him in blankets. I pulled the thick, wool blankets from the storage closet, then held the man up while the short ramp I had built for this purpose was slid under his shoulders and covered in pillows.

I volunteered to sit with the man. He had his eyes closed, and I thought he was asleep until he spoke.

"So, you're a priest, eh? No, don't bother to deny it. Your Jesus does not like it when you lie."

My mind whirled, and it took me a minute to realize his eyes were open and dancing with a humor that should not have been there.

"How . . .?"

"I've been a rabbi for fifty-three years, boy. I have spent most of that time working with your priests, trying to get our flocks to behave themselves. I've learned to sniff out a priest. Don't worry. I won't rat you out."

"Tell me your name."

"I am Uri Berkowicz, formerly of the Josefov, recently of some forsaken frozen hell, where I became 057659." He pulled the neck of his shirt down to reveal a small, black tattoo. "And I am pleased to make the acquaintance of anyone with wool blankets."

He held out a work and age stained hand and gripped mine with the wiry strength of the aged.

"Tell me, boy. How long do I have?"

"The Doctor hasn't told me anything . . ." I started, but he held up the hand he still had out of the blankets.

"I told you not to lie to me. Rabbi Yehoshua doesn't like it."

"Who?"

"Rabbi Yehoshua ben Yosep. The one you all like to hang in your houses and churches. Macabre, really. Like bowing before a man in a noose. Gruesome."

I must have still looked confused, because his mood became less jovial.

"Jesus, boy. I'm talking about your Jesus. I thought they taught you about the world in your seminaries. Now, answer my question."

"A few days. A week at most."

He nodded his head, which set him to coughing. I helped him sit up until his breathing eased. When I eased him down, he had lost most of the color he had gained since coming into the warm room. His hand, so strong a moment before, was limp, and I tucked it back under the blanket.

"A week. It is odd, knowing the length of my days. A relief, if you must know."

"A relief to die?"

"Look outside, boy. Those men we left inside the fence are already dead. They just don't know when their bodies will join them. The spirits have left; only numbered corpses remain.

"My name remains. They cannot take anything more from me."

"I don't understand."

He closed his eyes, and I thought again that he was asleep.

"Sir?"

"They cannot kill me, because I am not here. The parts of me that matter left long ago. All that remains is a shell that is too stubborn to give up. I beat them, boy. I beat them. My wife died before all this ugliness started. They cannot take her from me. And my boy . . . my son. He is in America. The last letter I received was him telling me he was going to be married. I beat them. I won. They didn't kill me."

He smiled his way into sleep, and I retreated to my sweeping. I could not understand how someone could be so happy in a place like this. Death was everywhere around us, could come from any angle at any moment, and this old man was smiling and snuggling his way deeper under the blankets.

I thought he was mad.

He slept his way through the afternoon, and only woke when Mrs. Tasic brought him a bowl of her soup. I never asked what was in it, but she had dosed me with it one day when I spent too much time out in the cold, and I wouldn't discount its healing powers. She fed him herself, making sure he did not eat too much, too quickly.

I sat up with him that night. He told me about his wife and son, of growing up in Prague and how he followed his father as a Rabbi. He said he had tried to keep a picture of them with him, but it had been taken during an inspection before he came here. He could only describe his wife as "beautiful."

Dr. Golc examined him the next morning.

"What do you think, Doctor?"

"Your chest does sound a little better."

"A little sleep does wonders, but I don't think I'll be leaving this bed."

I don't think any doctor is prepared for a patient who gleefully announces his own probable death.

"Don't worry yourself, Doctor. Getting better is the worst thing that could happen to me. I tell you, it is a relief to know I won't die at a whim."

"I have to ask: how were you even able to walk into the tent yesterday?"

"Force of will, young Doctor. The body can do many things when it has no other choice. I was told to walk into your tent; I walked into your tent. If you had not brought me here, I would have walked out of your tent, too."

"If I hadn't brought you here, you would have died last night."

"That is probably true. But I've been surprised each morning for months at the opening my eyes. This morning might have been no different."

Dr. Golc was silent for a long while. Uri took his hand.

"Your instinct is to save. So is mine. Those men out there, inside the wire. I cannot save them. You cannot save them. You cannot even heal them."

"I cannot let them die."

"As I told your young friend last night: they are already dead. As am I."

Dr. Golc left him, but I stayed by the bed. Uri shook his head.

"He cannot see what has happened. He is a good man."

"He can see it, but he cannot accept it. Neither can I. There has to be something we can do to stop this."

"Are you suddenly a warrior? Are you going to pick up a gun and kill all the guards to set my fellows free?"

"No, I . . ."

"No is right. Your death would serve nothing. Our deaths would become meaningless. We cannot be saved. But we can be remembered. You can remember us, Priest."

"I will remember. I have no other choice."

"You're a good boy."

I left him to rest. I think he wanted to talk longer, but he had so little strength left in him. He was an odd man, this Rabbi.

12

The mine reopened while Rabbi Berkowicz was in our care. We did not get as many patients as we did before the mine became a slave-hold. Injuries we had once treated, even with on-site amputations, became death sentences. We were the only hospital around, and Kortig did not want us to waste resources his soldiers might need. A bullet was cheaper than a scalpel.

While most of the camp's attention was on the mine, Dr. Golc started his own war against Kortig. His first attack was on the camp kitchen. The camp cook was an old soldier who had started in the German Army during the last war. He walked with a cane and terrorized any soldier unlucky enough to be assigned kitchen duty. Rare was the day his staff went to bed without thin bruises across their shins.

Kortig had ordered that prisoners were to be fed only bread and a soup made from vegetable peelings left over from the mess hall. Dr. Golc sent me over to the kitchen one morning with a pocket full of envelopes for the cook. When I arrived, he ushered me in with uncommon gentleness.

"Did you bring something for me from Golc?"

I pulled out the packets and handed them to the cook.

"Good…good…do you know what any of these are?"

He poured the envelopes onto a plate. Each contained powders that looked like the residue I cleaned out of Dr. Golc's pestle.

"I have no idea. Medicine?"

"Bright boy. This one fights fevers; that brown one strengthens the liver; those two thicken the blood."

He pointed out each before he poured the powders into the soup.

"Those are ground up pills?"

"Some are. Others come from your Mrs. Tasic. Good woman, that one; knows her herbs. I had an aunt like her, always walking through the forest, picking plants to help the neighbors."

"Will it help them?"

"To be honest, boy, if I thought I could do it and not get caught, I would poison the whole lot. That's no life, out there."

"You would murder them?"

He shook his head and stirred the soup.

"I don't know if this will help them out there; but it will not hurt them."

After that, he shooed me out of the kitchen. As I went past the window, I saw him toss the envelopes into the fire under the soup.

I thought about what the cook said, about poisoning the prisoners. Rabbi Berkowicz thought the men in the pen were already dead. I could not agree with either of them; these were men, and I could not agree that killing them would be a mercy.

13

Rabbi Berkowicz lived for five days. When he spoke, he often had to pause to cough and gasp for breath. I sat with him and listened as much as his strength would allow. He never did explain what the signs were that told him I was a priest.

"You have the smell of a priest."

"I smell like candles and incense?"

"Hardly, boy. I have been around enough of you to nose you out. Even if you never wear the collar, you wear your priesthood like a suit of clothes."

"I thought it was a smell."

"Metaphors, boy. Didn't you ever learn what religion really is?"

"Belief in God?"

"That is faith, not religion. Religion is how we explain what we believe. We teach in metaphors and parables so people can understand their faith. Did you ever attend a Synagogue while you were in your Seminary?"

"No. But I did have a friend…" I had not thought of Abraham for a very long time.

"You should, if the Nazis don't kill us all. I've attended your church many times, and the differences are so small they aren't even worth mentioning. Think about what your Mass really is."

"It's the ceremony between a priest and God."

"If that were the case, why would the people be invited in? Is it a spectator sport?"

"No, of course not."

"Do you know what we do on the Sabbath?"

"You pray with your family, right?"

He tried to answer, but was interrupted by a long coughing fit. I helped him sit up and held a cloth to his mouth. When I took it away, it was spotted with blood. He lay back for a few minutes with his eyes closed.

"Yes, but there is something else we do. We eat. The Sabbath starts with the meal at sundown, when a family comes together and shares food and blessings with each other. We share bread, share wine, pray to God. Sound familiar? What you do at Mass, we do with our families and friends. We gather together and share a meal. Yours has become mostly symbolic, but they are the same.

"Don't worry yourself sick over it. Most people never think about the connections. Most don't even remember that your Jesus was a Jew; or that the Last Supper was a Passover meal. We have the outward ceremonies because people respond to ceremonies and symbols. But what they symbolize is the same: community, faith, peace.

"You are going to see even more if you look for it. All over the world, people do the same things, for the same reasons, but only the outward symbols are different."

"But are they all worshipping God? What about all those people in India and China that worship whole pantheons?"

"Let me answer your question with a question I want you to think about: Would God, the loving God we share, create billions of people who have never heard of Him, just to cut them off from His love? We believe the world has been around for nearly six thousand years. Do you know how many people have never heard of Jews? How many in history have never heard of Jerusalem?"

"Then why does everyone believe they are the right ones?"

The old man started to smile, but it turned into a gasping cough. When he recovered, his voice was barely a whisper.

"Everyone wants to feel special."

Rabbi Uri Berkowicz died in his sleep that night.

14

The bodies lay in neat rows. I could not count them all, but I knew they all watched me, and they were all dead. I walked between the rows and tried to look into their faces, but they had none. I tried to get closer, but they stayed just out of reach. I heard a sound behind me and turned around. A man in a uniform pointed a gun at me. I yelled for him to stop, but he pulled the trigger.

The gunshots woke me. I sat up in my bed, unsure if what I heard was real or from the same nightmare I'd had since I escaped Lidice. The shouts brought me from my room, and I heard another gunshot. The nightmare followed me.

I had lived through the entire War without witnessing a battle. I wished that fact had remained.

Cover the flanks! Machine guns to the front! Mortars, fire at 100 meters!

The Doctor stood in the door to the ward. I ran up to him and looked over his shoulder at the flash-lit compound.

Get a message to Headquarters: River crossing at this position. Need reinforcements.

The soldiers I could see loosely ringed the hospital, their backs to us. A one-armed silhouette went from position to position, shouting orders.

Look for muzzle flashes in the trees. Mark their positions.

A large form broke away from one of the squads and ran to the hospital.

"Doctor. We have a problem."

"What the devil is going on, Feldwebel? What are you shooting at?"

"That is the problem, sir. There isn't anyone out there. It is theRittmeister: He's gone mad!"

"What do you mean?"

"He thinks he's back in Russia. I was with him when he lost his arm. We were trying to stop a river crossing of Mongol infantry, and he was wounded. He's back at that battle now!"

Doctor Golc stared at the soldier for a moment, then turned and pulled me by my sleeve into the pharmacy. He rooted through the shelves, mumbling the names of the few drugs we had available.

"Lumin…lumin…where's the damn…AHA! Got you! Boy! Come here. Get me two syringes."

I brought the instruments over, and Golc quickly loaded them both from the small bottle.

"Alright, boy, I need your full attention. We need to stick Kortig with this to stop him." He gave me one of the syringes. "Now, all you have to do is jab this into his ass and push down the plunger. I'll go first, but if I can't get to him, you'll need to do it. If I do get to him, hold off on using yours. We don't want to kill him, just put him to sleep. Got all that?"

I nodded. We went back into the ward where the Feldwebel waited. Golc waved him over and told him the plan.

"I would be grateful if you would grab his arm when we reach him, Feldwebel."

"Sir?"

"He still has his pistol, doesn't he?"

"Yes, sir."

"I'd rather he didn't shoot me. The lad here isn't up to surgery yet, and I don't fancy operating on myself."

"I see, sir. I will try. Will this make the Rittmeister forget?"

"He will probably think this is all a dream."

"Good. I'd rather not have him remember my part in this."

"Are we ready? Remember, boy, keep your syringe in reserve unless I fail to jab him with mine. And do your best not to get shot."

The Feldwebel led us out the door and into the dark. Kortig had his pistol pointed at one of the squads as he ordered them to throw their grenades towards an enemy only he could see. One soldier was motionless on the ground, and the others were throwing as fast as they could. The grenades fell into the prisoner pen, where the few flimsy buildings were already alight. A section of the fence blew apart as one grenade fell short.

The Feldwebel walked right up to Kortig and saluted.

"Message from Headquarters, sir!"

Kortig turned towards the Feldwebel, who locked his hand around the Rittmeister's wrist and thrust his hand and pistol skyward. Dr. Golc stepped up and lifted the Rittmeister's tunic skirt high enough to use the needle, but Kortig twisted and clipped the Doctor in the head with the stump of his missing arm. The Doctor dropped his syringe to grab Kortig around the waist.

"Now, boy! Do it now!'

I thrust my needle through the seat of Kortig's pants and pressed the plunger. Kortig stiffened at the intrusion, then slumped into the arms around him.

"Bring him to the hospital, Feldwebel. We need to check to see what damage has been done."

Without Kortig, the gunfire quickly quieted. The Doctor knelt next to the soldier on the ground, but did not examine him for long after one of the others shone a lantern on him. The soldier with the lamp had tears on his face.

"He tried to stop the Rittmeister. None of us thought he would shoot his own men."

Dr. Golc closed the dead man's eyes.

The soldiers moved away, and I saw where they had been throwing their grenades. The prisoner compound was on fire, and all the buildings were destroyed. They hadn't been sturdy to begin with, and the bombs and gunfire had created hell.

Nothing moved inside the fence. Kortig's junior officer came up to the Doctor and saluted.

"What in God's name do you think you're doing, boy? I'm not an officer."

"Sir, you are the highest ranking person in the camp right now. I need orders for the men."

"Orders? Here's an order: Tell the men to put out those fires and bring any survivors up to the hospital. Then, you can explain to me just what the hell you all were doing, shooting into the prisoner compound."

"Sir, the Rittmeister ordered us to fire. We fired."

I ran down to the prison gate, the Doctor behind me. The sentries stood at their posts, but they looked at the carnage. I tried the gate, but the metal was too hot from the fires for me to touch. I kicked the gate several times while the soldiers just stood there.

"Help me! We have to get them out of there!"

One of them shook his head as if to clear it, then set his rifle down. He held me back, then kicked the gate near the hinge three times. The bolts ripped out of the wood and the gate flew inward. I ran through the hole.

Closer to the fires, I could see what I had only imagined from the outside. A bare foot lay on its side, independent of any leg.

The prisoner dorms were the only buildings inside the fence, and they had born the brunt of the attack. I tried to enter, but the fire was too much. I couldn't see through the smoke, so I screamed when a hand grabbed my ankle. A man pulled himself out of the building.

It had to be a man. Its skin was blackened. It was naked and hairless, and dragged itself by its arms, while its legs were motionless and twisted. When I tried to turn it, him, on his back, the skin on his shoulders came off on my hands. But he could not scream.

The Doctor had followed me into the compound, and he saw what remained of the man that clutched at my leg.

"Dear God! He's . . ."

"You have to help him! We have to! Help me move him. We'll get him up to the hospital."

The Doctor looked at the man, then at me. He knelt down by the man's head.

"Look away, lad. You don't want to see this."

His eyes were hard and pleading at the same time while he held my gaze. I nodded and turned away.

I tried to pretend I heard twigs snapping.

When it was done, the Doctor pulled me away from the structure. It collapsed before we made it back to the gate. We did not bring anyone with us.

No one else had entered the prisoner compound.

15

The Feldwebel carried Kortig into the hospital and put him in a cot. When we came through the door, he was pulling off Kortig's boots. The Doctor checked his patient while I helped the Feldwebel strip him. I pulled off his gun belt and the Feldwebel replaced the pistol in its holster. The Doctor's office was the safest place to store the weapon, so I carried the belt through the door.

I set the whole outfit on the desk and noticed the leather box Kortig wore in front of his holster had flipped open. I reached to close it, but saw what looked like a scrap of fur inside. I lifted the flap and looked inside, but I could not make sense of what I saw. I dumped the contents onto the desk.

It was the mummified remains of a mouse.

16

Doctor Golc and the Feldwebel spent the rest of the night at Kortig's side, whether to restrain him or revive him I could not tell. At first light, the Feldwebel stood.

"I must report this. Please, don't leave him to wake up alone. I fear for his mind."

Doctor Golc had me sit with Kortig while he made a few notes and tried to sleep, with strict instructions to call for him if Kortig woke up. My job was to keep him calm and from hurting himself until the Doctor could check him.

I looked at Kortig. Here was a killer, a murderer. His sins were not hidden. Could I forgive him if he asked? Did he even see what he had done as sin?

I prayed as I sat next to Kortig. I did not even have a rosary, but I ran through the prayers, using my fingers instead of beads. When I finished, I found Kortig's eyes open and on me.

"Do you pray for me? Or for yourself?"

I stood to get the Doctor, but Kortig raised his stump, the only part of him not strapped to the bed.

"Stay for a moment. Answer the question."

"I pray for everyone."

"You do not think your prayers are wasted?"

"They are mine to waste."

Kortig closed his eyes and lay back on the pillow. I thought he was asleep again, but he spoke.

"Go and get the Doctor. Maybe he can explain why I am here."

I ran to the Doctor's office and found him asleep at his desk, pen still in hand. I shook his shoulder and brought him into the ward.

"Ahh, Doctor. So good to see you. A fine morning, wouldn't you say? Why the hell am I strapped down on a cot in your hospital?"

"Good morning, Rittmeister Kortig. It seems you went insane last night, and I thought it best to bring you here."

"What are you talking about? Release me at once!"

"I can't do that. What can you tell me about last night?"

"Last night? What do you mean?"

"Do you remember what you did last night?"

"I ate dinner alone, then retired to my quarters to read until I fell asleep. Then I woke up here."

"Did you have any dreams?"

"Dreams? What do dreams have to do with anything?"

"Please, just answer the question. Did you dream?"

Kortig stared at the Doctor for a minute, then sighed and relaxed.

"I only ever have one dream. About the night I lost …"

"About the night you lost your arm?"

"Yes." It was barely more than a whisper.

"And did you have that dream last night?"

"Yes."

"How long ago did you lose your arm?"

"Two years."

"And how long have you been back on duty?"

"Six months. This was my first command since. I asked to come back to serve the Fatherland."

"Did you talk to anyone about your dreams before?"

"Of course not! I am not one of the insane."

"I don't think you are, either. But you are not whole."

"Whole? Is that a joke, Doctor?"

"I don't mean your body. I mean your mind."

"I told you, I'm not insane."

"No, you're not insane. But you did kill one of your own men last night, and ordered the rest of your troops to fire into the prisoner compound."

"What?"

"Yes. You don't have any prisoners anymore."

"Who did I kill?"

"I don't know his name. A corporal, I believe. I think he tried to disobey your orders to throw grenades at the prisoners. After you shot him, the rest did what you wanted."

Kortig lay with his eyes closed for several moments.

"That is good. Orders should be obeyed."

Kortig's words hung until Doctor Golc stood up and walked away.

17

Kortig lay in the hospital for a week, restrained at night. Several times he woke me with screams he did not remember in the morning. We did not sedate him again.

On the last day, two officers arrived at the hospital and had Mrs. Tasic, the Doctor, and myself driven into town. The two silent soldiers who stayed with us stood outside the only remaining café in Nikde, impervious to the aromas of baking bread and weak coffee.

Kortig's bed was empty and stripped of blankets when we were allowed to return. One of the officers remained behind, seated at the Doctor's desk when we were ushered in.

"Good Afternoon. My name is Major Baader, and this is now my command."

"Where is my patient?"

"Rittmeister Kortig has been reassigned for the good of the Fatherland. I would like to thank you for your service concerning his health."

"He was in no state to be released."

"That is no longer your problem, Doctor. Now, let us discuss this hospital of yours. I have been looking through your records, Doctor. You seem to be working with very little here."

"Supplies are difficult to come by, this far from any front."

"This is true. But this is also a military hospital, and as such it should be better supplied. Please make up a basic list of what medications you need to care for, say, 400 men. Give it to my aide by 1700 tomorrow and we'll see about getting you back in the business of medicine."

"400 men? Are you bringing in more soldiers?"

"Hmm? Oh, no, there is already a full compliment for a camp this size. But we still need to work this mine. So, we will bring in workers."

"I saw what happened to your last batch of workers."

"Oh yes. The accident. Nasty business, that."

"Accident? That was murder!"

"I am not here to debate the methods used to execute condemned prisoners. I am here to run a mine. Now, if there is nothing else, I must get to my own work. Please let me know if there is anything you need. We will work together."

The Major stood. When he reached the door, he paused and looked back.

"Can you spare your assistant for a few minutes, Doctor? I'm sure he knows the camp, and I would like a tour from someone who doesn't fear for their career."

The Doctor nodded and I followed the Major into the camp.

The soldiers had spent the last several days cleaning up the remains of the prisoner compound. They didn't do anything so noble as recover bodies. Instead, a large pit was dug in the middle of the fenced in area and everything was tossed in and covered with dirt. They drove trucks over the mound in an attempt to flatten it.

The Major had a fast stride, and I had to hurry to keep up with him. He did not look at the camp, but led me toward the mine entrance, where no one but guards had come in a week. We went past the guards and entered the mouth of the mine.

When we were several yards in, the Major stopped.

"This is far enough. We should be able to talk here."

My heart quickened.

"What would you like to talk about?"

"I would like to talk about the pouch you have hidden under the floorboards in your room. I would like to talk about what I found in that pouch."

"What pouch is that, sir?"

"Please don't play games with me. You don't have the face for it."

The Major was unable to stand still while he talked. His hands traced the pick-marks in the walls. He frowned at the black smudges on his fingers and wiped them on a handkerchief. He tucked it back in his pocket and brought his hand back out with something in it.

"This war has made everyone so very careful. The wrong word, the wrong name, the wrong family, the wrong religion, the wrong anything, and everything ends in misery and pain. We live in a time of lies. Tell me the truth of your lies. Confess to me."

He crossed himself as he spoke the last words and I saw what was in his hand.

A violet stole.

For a moment, I was sure it was my own. But this one was longer than mine, and fringed with gold braid. The Major kissed the cross at the nape and draped it around his shoulders.

"Confess and be forgiven."

18

There is no feeling quite like finding a brother where none should have been. I had wandered alone for the last year. I had borne witness to the horrors man can inflict upon man. I had seen death and fire and the destruction that comes to the human body from cold and calculated cruelty. I had seen Hell.

And I wasn't alone.

I had seen no other priest since I left Brno. I went through Christmas and Easter, unable and unworthy of the sacraments, unshriven, unclean. I said Mass in the quiet of my head, but without a confessor, I feared for my soul. I blessed the dying, but was unblessed.

All this I confessed.

The sin of Pride, giving what was not mine to give.

The sin of Cowardice, hiding from those I feared.

The sin of Lies.

The sin of Hate.

The sin of Inaction.

The sin of Despair.

I confessed for over an hour, kneeling on the rocks and boards between the cart rails, my face streaked with coal dust where I wiped away my tears. My knees bled from the sharp stones.

When I finished, I fell back, exhausted. Baader stood over me and pronounced my penance: to continue my work. I looked up at him, and he must have read the confusion in my eyes.

"You have not truly sinned, little brother. Not in any way that matters. You are doing extraordinary work in extraordinary times. You have done the best you can. And, yes, you have broken a few rules. But the fact that you thought the work was more important shows you are starting to learn an important truth."

"But these are all sins! Mortal sins!"

"Normally, yes. But did you do any of those to gain anything for yourself?"

"I ran and hid to protect myself."

"Self-preservation is not a sin. The one thing we do not need is a martyr. And you did not just do it for yourself. You bore witness. You do so here, as well. And witness is a heavy weight to bear."

"I gave sacraments without absolution."

"Would you have sent those men into the dark alone?"

"I did not stop Kortig."

"From the report I saw, you did stop him. You were the one who sedated him."

"I don't mean then. He killed a boy." I told him about the trial.

"How would you have stopped him?"

"I…"

"Exactly. The only guilty man there was Kortig."

"He killed sick prisoners."

"Oh, yes. I read about that in the Doctor's files. Do you know what he said about the prisoners Kortig executed? The words 'pneumonia' 'tuberculosis' and 'epidemic' came up more than once. And your little hospital could not have done anything but prolonge their pain. Those men would have died, and would have spread illness in the camp."

"Are you trying to excuse what Kortig did?"

"No. He is a murderer, and, unless I miss my guess, quite insane. But I am looking at reality. You and the Doctor were able to save a few of those poor men for a little longer. You treated them as humans."

"So, what is this truth I am supposed to learn?"

"Hmm? Oh, yes. The truth is, everything is deeper than we think. You were worried about surface sins, the sort of thing I'm sure was drilled into you. But now you are out in the world, and in a world ripped apart by the worst sort of Evil humans can create. The Rules are nice to follow in times of peace. But it is more important to understand the spirit of the rules and abide by that than worry about details."

"I'm not sure I understand. Why teach the Rules if we can ignore them when they are inconvenient?"

"Let me see if I can explain. One of the ideas we inherited from the Jews was the idea of the Holy Sabbath. The day of rest, when we are not supposed to work. Would you expect a Doctor to turn away a patient on the Sabbath?"

"No, of course not."

"Would you expect a mother to not feed her children on the Sabbath? The spirit of the Sabbath is to rest, to spend time with family, to contemplate God. The reality is, people still need to eat, animals need to be cared for, patients need treatment. You are out where adherence to the letter of the Rule is impossible. But you have kept the spirit with you."

"I still feel better after Confession."

"As you should. And when you come back to civilization, you will need to follow the Rule again. But remember; you are doing God's work, and that cannot be a sin."

He stood to leave, but I stopped him with a hand on his arm.

"I have to know: how is this possible?" I gestured to his uniform.

Baader looked down at himself and gave a laugh.

"You mean, how can I be a German officer and a priest?"

I nodded.

"Of those three things, German, officer, and priest, only one is true. I'm Swiss, and I've never worn a uniform before. My mother was from Berlin, and I learned her German as a child. My superiors in Bern wanted to know what was going on; I spoke the right type of German. A few forgeries, a little bribery, and I became an Officer in Hitler's stupidity. From there to here, all I did was follow orders."

"It was coincidence?"

"Not quite. I came across Kortig's file a few years ago. There are not all that many zealots to Hitler's cause, but Kortig stood out. Most men with injuries like his would have been retired; he stayed because he's a believer. When the report of the massacre here came up to headquarters, I volunteered to come."

"But you're a priest…"

"I am. And when this is over, I will report what I have seen to my Bishop and take up my cassock again. Just as you will."

"I don't know if I can just go back."

"It's part of who you are, Jan; you won't be able to just stop."

He started towards the mouth of the cave, then turned back.

"I'm trusting you with my secret only because you're a fellow priest, Jan. You need to understand just how much danger we're both in; if anyone finds out about us, we die. It's that simple: we die. No one can know about me: not your Mrs. Tasic; not Doctor Golc; no one."

He left me with myself while he replaced the kindly Swiss priest with the German officer. I did not leave the mine until dark.

19

Reconstruction of the camp took well into the cool of autumn. Baader kept the soldiers working while he slowly transferred the cleverest among them to other units, replaced with men too stupid to ask questions. The first to go was Kortig's Feldwebel. I made sure to shake his hand before he left.

I watched the rebuilding progress as the prisoner pen once again took shape. The three sections that faced the road, the camp, and the mine entrance were all built with sturdy posts and row after row of barbed wire. When the three sides were completed, a second fence was built around the first, with a path wide enough for two guards to walk side by side between the fences.

On the fourth side, the narrow side that faced the mountain, a solid wall of wooden planks made up the wall. The thick boards were bolted to the poles, only a few meters from the solid rock of the mountain. There was no room for the guard path, so the soldiers would have to walk back and forth, rather than around the whole pen.

I conversed with Baader regularly, under the pretext of accepting delivery of supplies. Mrs. Tasic ran out of room in the pharmacy, so construction on the camp was paused for a few days to build an addition to her specifications.

The only patients we had were uniformly young and healthy soldiers, who required very little doctoring. With Baader's permission, Doctor Golc and I took over an abandoned printer's shop in town and provided care three days out of the week. Mrs. Tasic remained at the mine for any emergency, so we needed a nurse in town.

Nikde was a starved, occupied town. Hundreds of people left during Kortig's reign, and the ones that remained survived on kitchen gardens and support jobs for the soldiers. Nothing thrived, but the best-fed people in town were the cobblers, seamstresses, and prostitutes. Money was rare and useless. Eggs, butter, bread, and meat were the currency of need.

I did not know the circumstances by which Golc found our new assistant, Lida. When I met her, she was dressed very primly, her dark hair pulled back into a severe bun, her eyes lowered as Dr. Golc introduced her. She was close to my own age, and reminded me of the girls Vavrinec and I danced with, lifetimes ago.

When Dr. Golc left us alone, she told me about her last job. Nikde had a brothel long before the Nazis arrived, mostly to serve the miners who had no wives waiting for them at home. When the mine first closed, the brothel did as well, although the madam stayed in the town. When the soldiers came in, she reopened her doors. Lida could either starve or take the only work open to her. According to her story, she did not stay long; her first customer was her last.

She had left a tooth behind when she escaped the brothel, and her nose aimed slightly left, but her mind was quick enough, behind a veil of chatter, to learn all Golc could teach her and improve on most of it. Between visits, Lida would clean the clinic and guard the precious supply of medicines I carried down the hill. She gave up her room in the brothel on the same day she left, so I helped her set up a room for herself on the second floor of the building, just a cot and some shelves for her things. As a gift, I gave her a handful of candles and a book I had finished.

Our schedule was never set in stone. I came alone to the clinic one afternoon, as Doctor Golc and Mrs. Tasic were busy with an emergency appendectomy for one of the new soldiers. I was only supposed to check on the supplies and pass along the message from Doctor Golc to anyone who came in.

Lida was alone. She stood up and smiled at me when I walked in.

"You're the first person to come through that door all day. Are you here to keep me company?"

"I'm supposed to tell anyone who comes that the Doctor won't be in today."

"Well, now everyone here knows, and since you did such a good job, you can stay and talk to me. Have you ever been to Prague?"

"No, I've never had the chance..."

"I want to go to Prague when the war is over. I want to see all the dresses the rich women wear there. Or Paris. Do you think Paris will still be there when the war is over?"

In the few weeks I had known Lida, I had contributed little to any conversation.

"Did you like the book I gave you?"

"Oh, yes, but it didn't make much sense to me. Can you really bring dead tissue back to life with electricity? We used to have an electric light at home, but whenever I touched it, I would see a little bolt of lighting jump from the switch to my hand. It hurt. I would think something that brought life would feel good, not hurt."

"I don't think you should take it word for word. I remember my teacher telling us that Mary Shelley thought of this story after an opium dream."

"Opium? I wonder what that would do to me. I don't think I want to have dreams about bringing scary creatures to life. Would you like some tea? It's not real tea, just some dried flower petals, but it tastes good. I wish I had some sugar. Do you have a fiancé?"

"What? I ... no, I don't have a fiancée."

"I had a fiancé, but he left with the army and didn't come back. I don't think disappearing is good for a relationship. If he comes back and I'm already married, it will be his own fault. I certainly didn't ask him to go be a soldier. I wanted him to open a chocolate shop. Every town should have a chocolate shop. Did you happen to bring any extra penicillin?"

"I think I brought some. I don't think I would call it extra."

"Well, I have enough doses here to last quite a while, if everyone agrees to stay healthy, and my cousin told me he would trade sugar, flour, chocolate, and books for penicillin. I thought it would be nice if we could offer some of those things to any patients that have to stay here overnight. And I wouldn't mind a chocolate now and then either."

"Wait a second. Your cousin is black market?"

"Oh, yes. He's really clever. He managed to stay out of the war, and always knows the news. He told me the Russians are pushing the Germans back and a bunch of Jews destroyed a Nazi camp in Hungary or someplace. Or maybe they just escaped, I don't know. Anyway, if there is something you want, just let me know and he will trade for medicine."

"Can he get messages through without the Nazis finding out?"

"Oh, sure. He takes letters from me to my mother all the time. He knows everybody! Why? Do you want to write to someone?"

"I don't know yet. Maybe."

"It wouldn't cost you much. Did you bring me a new book to read?"

"I brought one, but I didn't know if you would like it. It's all about Greek myths."

"Oh, that should be good. Lots of different stories, right?"

"Yes."

Lida clapped her hands and grabbed me in an embrace that made me very aware of my vows.

"You really should get a fiancée. Maybe you could be my fiancé. We wouldn't have to get married, but you could bring me flowers when you visit, and we could talk about books. Oh, and if you are my fiancé, you can kiss me."

Lida grabbed my shoulders and planted her lips directly on my own. Her eyes were closed, but mine were so far open they hurt. Her lips tasted of berries I'd eaten as a child, and she smelled of soft talcum. She let me go and I fell off the bench we shared.

"There. Now we're betrothed. You should have brought me a ring, but this has all been so sudden. We can worry about that later."

I stammered some sort of reply, although I would not swear I made any sense in the least. I walked up the hill slowly, and often touched my fingers to my lips.

20

I told Baader about my "fiancée" when I met him for one of our discussions. I did not find his laughter very charitable.

"Don't worry so much. This could be a good thing. Nobody would suspect a priest of having a fiancée. And, as long as you behave yourself, you won't break any of the rules."

"But I don't know how to be a fiancé!"

"Just do like she said. Bring her some flowers when you visit."

"You're not helping!"

"Oh, calm down. I have a wife in Prague. It really is one of our best disguises."

"How can you have a wife?"

"She's a nun. Unlike you, I'm underground because I'm supposed to be. She came with the assignment."

"Surely you don't …"

"No, we don't. I have grown very used to sleeping on the floor over the last few years."

"And nobody suspects?"

"What would they suspect? She's from Switzerland, like me, and speaks perfect German. She socializes with the other officer's wives and gains far more information than I ever could. In the evenings, we go to the Officer's Club, or to the cinema. We hold hands, and walk arm-in-arm down the street. It's a disguise, as much as my uniform and her silk dresses."

"Lida is not a nun. I can't use her like that."

"I don't think you're in any danger where she is concerned. I am fairly sure she just wants someone to talk to who doesn't remind her of her old life."

"I cannot imagine her in a brothel."

"Is she missing a tooth?"

"How did you know that?"

"It was one of my men who knocked it out. He's the one who has been cleaning the latrine every day for the last month. I think he understands now that I don't approve of his behavior. Anyway, from what my men told me about the incident, she wasn't exactly defenseless. My man was her first client, and as bad as he hit her, she was able to damage him in return. I don't know exactly what she did, but he wasn't interested in a return visit for a few weeks after their encounter."

I took flowers on my next trip to the clinic. Two women were in labor when we arrived. The flowers stayed on the bench next to the door where I dropped them.

21

Prisoners returned, inevitably. Baader could not avoid filling his camp forever, although he was able to put it off for months with construction. But we all knew a train would come, and it came with the first snowfall.

Doctor Golc insisted on meeting the train at the railhead to check the prisoners for signs of disease. Baader agreed to hospitalize any prisoners Doctor Golc chose.

The officer in charge of the train marched to where we stood. His salute came with the smile of someone telling a dirty joke.

"Here are your prisoners, Major. They're a healthy lot. Should be able to work hard for a long time."

He signaled the train and the doors slid open.

The men who emerged were not a uniform group. Some were tall and blonde; others had a darker cast to their skin. Their clothes were the same striped outfits of all Grey Men. But there were no yellow stars. One man, larger than all the rest, walked with his hands bound behind him and armed soldiers on either side. His face skewed around a long scar and his eyes did not track in the same direction. After him walked a much smaller man, whose face darted from side to side. He reminded me of a rat, his shoulders hunched, his bony hands always held in front of him.

Green triangles were sewn to their chests. Baader rounded on the officer.

"What is the meaning of this?"

"This is your workforce, Major. Headquarters noted the Jews didn't last very long, and their output from the mine was never up to standards. All of these men have only recently come into our hands, and they don't have that Jewish aversion to physical labor."

"You brought me criminals!"

"Only some of them. The rest are perverts. Maybe you can sweat the indecency out of them."

Baader turned away from the platform and bellowed for his Feldwebel. Doctor Golc and I walked through the ranks of the prisoners. Two men showed signs of fever and we sent them to the waiting Mrs. Tasic. The rest were healthy. They were moved to the fenced area and I went to Baader's office.

Baader had one of the few telephones in the area, and he was using it in full voice.

"Sir, this is unacceptable! I am not set up to contain criminals. My men are soldiers, not gaolers!

....

"No, sir, I do not think my men can handle this.

....

"No, they are fine men, but they are not trained…

....

"I'm not trained for that either, sir.

....

"Yes, sir.

....

"I will do my best, sir."

He gently set the handle back in the cradle, then threw the entire telephone through the window behind his desk.

"Merde."

I stood in his doorway.

"For celibate men, we have just been well and truly fucked."

"What is going on? What is wrong with the men in the camp?"

"Whom did you have here before? With Kortig, I mean. Who were the prisoners?"

"Czechs, Slavs, Poles."

"All Jews, yes?"

"I think so."

"That is what I planned for. You saw all those renovations to the camp, yes? They weren't to make the fence stronger. Quite the opposite. A few weeks from now, you and I were going to slip into the forest and remove some of the boards from the back section of the fence; they're only bolted on, and we could remove enough for people to squeeze through in just a few seconds. I have a cache of supplies, maps, and weapons buried in the trees. You were going to lead them out of here."

"So, what is the problem? I'm willing to go."

"The problem is, I cannot let these men go."

"What?"

"The men with the green triangle? Those men are criminals. The same criminals that would be in prison in any civilized country; murderers, rapists, smugglers, thieves. Men even the Nazis couldn't leave to wander the streets free."

A discreet knock interrupted whatever he was going to say, and an aide entered with a thick stack of paper. Baader half-heartedly returned the salute and gestured for the aide to leave. His eyes roamed over the top page.

"This is exactly what I mean. Jean-Marie du Leon: convicted of torturing and murdering farm families in France. Here's another, convicted of looting a church in Berlin."

"Why would they send men like that here?"

"I have my enemies. When I took this job, we had to create a career history to put me in the right place. We did a good job. Too good. I was promoted ahead of someone who really wanted the job I had in Prague, in charge of trade. It is a wonderful job for whoever is in charge. I could get anything I wanted, and if some things disappeared, it was up to me to report it. If I didn't, nobody knew anything was missing. Now, that man is in charge of prisoner transfers in this part of Europe. I'm sure he saw this as a chance to get back at me."

"So, what are you going to do?"

"I have no idea. I came here with this plan, minus the part about you leading them. I was going to do that myself, but with you here, I thought I could do it a second time myself and get twice as many people out. Now, though…"

He stood and we both looked through the hole in the window from his telephone.

Snow fell.

22

The Jewish prisoners had been starved into docility. The new prisoners were strong and healthy. And violent. Separated by language, united only in situation, angry factions sprang up along national lines: the Poles hated the French, who hated the Belgians, and everyone hated the Germans.

And, for the first time since the real miners had abandoned the dark, the hospital was busy. Not from mine accidents, although those came in as well. Now we spent our days setting broken bones and stitching stab wounds from the daily fights that erupted for any or no reason.

I had little to do in my private war of blessings. The few men who died did so in the prison yard or dorms, and were simply buried without ceremony. The ones who made it to the hospital were wounded, but not fatally. Doctor Golc treated them, but without the tenderness he had for the miners and prisoners who came before. The bottle of slivovitz stayed in his office.

My visits to Lida took a much less medical aspect. I could supply some medicines, but with the Doctor busy at the camp, few patients came to our clinic. What I did bring slid into the Black

Market, replaced with a few luxuries Lida distributed around the town. She showed me her storeroom one day, and I saw boxes of everything from perfume to horseshoe nails.

We became friends. She still called me her fiancé, but only to watch me blush. She had spotted me for an innocent, and took far too much delight in that fact. We talked. We explored the town, home to neither of us. She told me her story, and I told her one that was close enough to the truth without exposing my priesthood.

We traded books. She could read French, and wanted me to read a book she had received from her cousin, but my French was about as good as my Mongolian. She read a few passages by a man named Henry Miller, but had to stop when she couldn't hold the book and laugh at my reactions at the same time. The things some people do to each other!

When I returned from one of these visit, I noticed something new in the prisoner pen: the wooden section of the wall closest to the mountain now had a tall fence of barbed wire between it and the open yard. I watched as a pair of guards circled the entire pen.

23

Spring bloomed, and my trips to town became more frequent. The civil postal service resumed, although under tight control, but Doctor Golc was able to make contact with some colleagues, as long as they were within the German state. I was tempted to write home, but I still didn't know what to say. I could not explain my disappearance, and I did not want anyone to worry more about me.

I continued to meet with Lida, and I let her get closer to me than anyone had in years. I found her, one Tuesday in May, near the town fountain, once a work of art but now a necessity for anyone who wanted fresh water. She had drawn water to wash the clinic linens, and I carried her buckets back. While she heated the water, we talked about the translation of Sherlock Holmes stories I left with her last time. She was adamant that Watson was the true hero of the stories.

"He's the one who does all the work. He looks for clues. All Holmes does is smoke and wait for the information so he can take credit later."

"But everything Watson does is *for* Holmes. He is almost a servant!"

"Why can't a servant be a hero?"

"He can, but Watson isn't! He would never figure out how everything fits together without Sherlock."

We dissolved into giggles over the absurdity of our discussion. She stopped first. When I regained control of myself, Lida was much closer than she had been before. Her face was almost touching mine.

"Why don't you ever kiss me?"

"I did, once. Anyway, I thought I wasn't your fiancé anymore."

"That time doesn't count. I kissed you. You didn't kiss me. You don't need to be my fiancé to kiss me. Sometimes, a woman just wants to be kissed."

"I…"

She moved through the remaining space and her lips came across mine. She smelled of soap and lilacs, and her lips tasted of the wildflower tea she brewed every morning. Her eyes were open and locked on mine, waiting. Our lips touched, but we did not kiss, yet.

I could not help myself. I pressed my lips hard on hers, and I saw her eyes close just before my own. Her lips parted, and we tasted each other's breath. Her hands wound through my hair and knocked my cap to the floor.

She pulled back from me and gave me a look, almost animalistic. I became prey, a rabbit before the wolf. But I was no rabbit. I looked at her mouth. I wanted another taste. Her lip swelled, a ripe fruit, just waiting to be bitten. She was both apple and Eve.

I trapped her lower lip between my teeth and tugged. Her eyes flew open, and when I released, her breath escaped in a sigh.

"You… What did you do to me?"

I grinned.

"Nothing you haven't done to me before."

She shifted her arms away from me and moved them to the buttons on the front of her dress. I watched her fingers; her long fingers. Her dress slipped off her shoulders, baring the startling white of her shift. Her face flushed as she toyed with the ribbon holding the flimsy garment in place.

"What are you..?"

She placed a finger across my lips, then replaced it with her own mouth.

"Shhhh."

She lifted my hands from her waist and placed them on her covered breasts. The heat of her skin burned my skin as I took up their weight. She leaned into me.

"I will never be a bride; no man will try to own me again. But I can offer myself to you as a wife to her husband."

The hard points of her nipples stabbed into my palms as she leaned into me. My hands moved over her flesh to the still-tied ribbons. I tugged first one, then the other, and the garment fell to her waist.

Her chest flushed in the shape of a large strawberry. A scar marred her stomach, the remains of long ago, before I knew her, a time that no longer mattered. She first covered, then presented her breasts with her hands, holding them towards me as a fine meal. I bent my head towards her nipple.

And stopped. I could not go further. I should not have gone this far. I backed away from her, my eyes locked on her. I forgot the large pot of now-boiling water behind me. Lida wore a question, but it fled as my back touched the brim of the pot and I let loose a howl.

I jumped forward and landed almost in her lap. She quickly checked my back for burns, but I had escaped any serious damage. Then she pushed me away from her.

"Why did you pull away?"

"I… I cannot do what you want."

"Why? You want to. I want to. Why stop?"

"Lida, I'm…"

"Is it because I was a whore? It was only one night, and I never got to the big moment. I'm still a virgin."

"No, nothing like that."

"I know I'm forward. Is that it?"

"Lida, please! I'm trying to tell you."

I kept my eyes on the floor. She had not covered anything.

"Will you look at me?"

I raised my eyes. I could not see her nudity, only her face.

"Now. Tell me."

"Lida, I'm a priest."

"A what?"

"I'm a priest. I'm in hiding, but I am a priest. And I cannot be what you want from me."

Lida's mouth dropped for several moments. Her face turned a different shade of red, and she spun to put her back to me while she pulled her clothes back into place.

"Oh, God. A priest? A real priest? And I just…"

"You just made me the most wonderful offer anyone ever has."

"I'm going to Hell!"

"No! Never say that."

"But I just showed you my…and I kissed…I was going to…"

"You did nothing wrong. I'm the one who lied. I'm the one who didn't tell you before."

"Can you forgive me?"

"There is nothing to forgive, Lida. You gave me a gift. That is all. It is one, sadly, I cannot accept. But there is nothing wrong in the offering."

"It is a sin! I tempted a priest! I looked at you with lust!"

"I don't think it was lust. I do love you, Lida. And you do draw up a passion in me. But it is not as base as lust."

"I am so ashamed."

This was going nowhere. I grabbed her wrists in one hand and raised her face with the other.

"Lida. You did not know. If I were the man I pretend to be, the man you thought you knew, I would not have said no. But, I couldn't do that to you. I couldn't lie to you anymore."

We sat, not touching, not talking, until the sunlight through the windows was sharp slanted. I stood.

"I can only ask your forgiveness, Lida. Will you?"

"I think I shouldn't. But I do. And I do love you, too. But I don't think I want to see you ever again."

I understood. I could offer no words here anymore. I reached out my hand to touch her hair, but stopped short. I could never touch her again.

24

The hospital was quiet. I had swept the floors, changed all the sheets, and polished everything that could stand the abuse; anything to shift the image of Lida from my mind. Every night, as I closed my eyes, I saw her: smiling, lovely, a gift in her eyes and in her hands. Too many times, I stopped myself from running down the mountain to find her, to throw everything away for her.

Doctor Golc had shut himself in his office and Mrs. Tasic was at the clinic with the medicines I could no longer convey. To calm prisoners, Baader had ordered a speaker system strung through the camp, and he had found a recording of Enrico Caruso arias, which only succeeded in making me sad. In his office, I confessed to Baader about Lida, but he only smiled and shook his head at me. He told me he could not absolve a sin that was never committed.

The shouts started out faint. The music screeched to a stop and a voice gave orders in German. Fights in the compound were common, and I stood in the doorway to see if we would have patients. I couldn't see exactly what was going on, but I could hear shouts of pain. I turned to fetch Doctor Golc, but he stood beside me already.

A shot came from one of the guard towers. Sadly, this happened nearly as often as the fights. The tower guards would disperse the prisoners with a warning shot. This time, the shot was answered with several shots from inside the fence. I turned to look at the Doctor and saw the blood drain from his face. He shoved me aside and ran towards the compound. I followed.

The prisoners had a gun. Maybe several. Two guards were wounded and one was dead by the time we reached the fence. The prisoners barricaded themselves in a buildings, the door closed. In the yard, two still forms.

We treated the two guards first. One had a shallow groove along his leg, the other's shoulder dripped with blood. We patched them up as well as we could and sent them up to the hospital. Mrs. Tasic would return soon, and she could tend them as well as the Doctor.

When we turned toward the gate, the guards moved to stop us. Doctor Golc face turned a vibrant shade of red as they blocked us.

"Get out of my way! Those men are injured, and we're going in to help them."

"Sir, no one is to enter the compound."

"If you don't move, I'm going to suture your mouth to the ass of a syphilitic whore!"

They moved.

The first man was dead, a hole through one eye and the back of his head far removed. The other man breathed. Doctor Golc knelt over him to check for wounds. The man's eyes popped open and he latched on to the Doctor with one arm while the other produced a pistol.

"Don't move. Don't yell. I'm going to stand up now, and we're all going into the barracks. Nod if you understand."

The pistol was at Doctor Golc's head: we followed directions. And went into the dark of the prisoner barracks.

Baader's plans for these buildings had not included long use. The only source of light came from the cracks left by poor construction and cheap materials. The faces were shadowed, but I could feel every pair of eyes on me.

The man who brought us in squatted down in front of the two of us.

"Here's the situation. We can't leave without getting our heads shot off. But I also heard some of the guards talk about what happened to the last batch of poor bastards you had here. Hopefully the chief out there thinks enough of you two to keep from pulling a repeat. Sound good?"

"You bastards! I came in here to help you, and this is how you repay me?"

"Oh, but you are helping us. Your job is to keep people alive, yes? Well, right now, you are keeping 148 men alive and whole. Good job, Doctor. That might be a record."

I cut in.

"You didn't need to do this. Major Baader would never order his men to massacre you like that."

"He's a Nazi, isn't he? Let me tell you something, kid. We may be criminals and murderers in here, but the worst of us pale compared to what I have seen the Nazis do. Place I was before this? Up in Poland? Whenever a train pulled in, anyone who wasn't healthy and strong was killed, gassed, as soon as they arrived. Thousands. Maybe millions. I couldn't count them all. And the whole place was covered in greasy ashes. Want to know why?

Because the Nazis, the ones just like your Major, had the bodies burned like they were scrap wood. So don't give me your story."

I couldn't tell them why I knew Baader wouldn't kill them. His men might, and had. An escape attempt months before resulted in three men executed before Baader could return from a meeting in Prague.

A shout reached us from outside. It was Baader.

"Release your hostages, and put down your weapons, and I promise there will be no reprisals!"

The prisoner in charge made his way to the door and opened it a crack.

"Can't trust you, sir. Heard too many stories. Seen too many things."

"What do you want?"

"Release us. Just open the gate and let us go."

"You know I can't do that."

"Then we have a problem. I suggest you go away and come up with a solution. Or we'll have to do something permanent to the Doctor here."

25

We sat.

The sun slanted, and we sat.

The stars rose, and we sat.

I did not sleep. I could not call anyone in the room innocent, but I could hear some of the men whisper to each other. And, of the few I could understand, I learned this was the plan of very few of the prisoners. The man who argued most strongly against the plan lay in the prison yard.

The sun rose, and Baader returned.

"You men in there! I'm ready to talk!"

The man in charge went back to the door.

"We're listening."

"I cannot simply let you go. But I can set a limit to your sentences. Any man who comes out now, with his hands in the air, will be released from this prison after two years of labor in the mine."

"You call that a compromise?"

"I have your records here. The least amount of time any of you were sentenced to is 25 years. So, yes, I call this a compromise."

"Give us a few minutes. Don't go anywhere." He shut the door.

The men inside shouted.

"Take the deal! Two years is nothing!"

"To hell with that! I want out, now!"

"Nous allons mourir!"

"Wer hat Sie verantwortlich?"

"Mitä on tekeillä?"

The debate collapsed into a shoving and shouting match, and Doctor Golc and I tried to take advantage of the situation. But, before we could reach the door, the man in charge regained order by shooting the loudest dissenter through the throat. He grabbed the Doctor and pulled him back to the middle.

"Oh, no, Doctor. We can't have you leaving us just yet. And the rest of you … shut your mouths and keep them that way. I'm really not interested in what any of you think. But, I do believe in letting every man choose his own destiny. So, if any of you want to take this offer, there is the door. Feel free to leave."

Doctor Golc stood with bulging eyes.

"If you were going to let them leave, why did you shoot that man? He wanted to take the offer!"

"Don't pity him, Doctor. He liked to rape little girls. Not exactly a loss in the world."

Nearly half the men walked out the door, hands above their heads. The leader had his ear to the door, waiting for something. But no sounds came from the outside.

"Huh. I was sure they would be executed as they left. Never thought I would see the day a Nazi kept his word."

I had to bite my cheek.

26

I lost all sense of time. It could have been afternoon, or evening, or even still morning. The dead man in the middle of the room had gone through the final human indignity, and the atmosphere inside the building was foul.

Doctor Golc's temper did not improve with time. He muttered curses through a wide variety of languages until he couldn't keep still any longer. He stood up and walked to the door.

"Where do you think you're going, Doctor?"

"I have two wounded patients in my hospital. I'm going to attend to them."

"You have courage, I must admit, Doctor. Now, please sit back down."

"You won't shoot me. You said it yourself: I'm your protection. If you kill me, they'll just storm in here and send the rest of you to hell."

"You really think so? What about your assistant?"

"They wouldn't shoot him."

"No, but I would. He is as much protection as you are. And less trouble. Now, sit down and keep quiet."

I went to them and tried to pull Doctor Golc back to where we sat. He shook off my hand. He gave me a smile and shook his head.

"No, lad. Go sit down. You'll be alright."

I backed away.

"I am going out there."

The leader put the gun to Doctor Golc's head.

"Don't make me do this, Doctor."

"I can't make you do anything." He stepped to the door.

I closed my eyes to the gunshot.

When I opened them again, Doctor Golc lay on his front, his head in a mess of blood and brains. I knelt beside him and turned him to his back. There was no hope for him.

I had my stole in my pocket, where I kept it anytime I was in the hospital ward. I pulled it out without thinking, and placed it around my neck. I had no oil, but I blessed Doctor Golc's eyes and mouth, throat, heart, and hands. I never did know what, if anything, the man had believed. But he had taught me and protected me, and I could not leave him.

I finished the prayers and put his hands on his chest. I could not make him look peaceful. I stood and faced the murderer.

His eyes widened. I did not know if it was fear or horror. It wasn't the death that bothered him. It was me.

"You're a ..."

"A priest. Yes, I am." And I hit him.

I had never hit someone before, not seriously. I had fought with other boys as any child would. But this punch came from somewhere much deeper than childhood anger. I hit the point of his chin and his head snapped back.

I picked up the gun he dropped and put it against his head.

"I could kill you now and send you straight to hell, damned for all eternity. You are a murderer of the worst kind: you kill for convenience. You killed the man who took me in."

I could smell the urine as it left his body. I stood over him for a very long time, my finger on the trigger.

"But I am not that man. I am a priest."

I threw the gun out the door. He sighed with relief and laid his head back. I stomped as hard as I could on his jaw.

None of the other prisoners had moved the whole time. Two of them had guns, but they left them in their belts. I turned to face them.

And they knelt. One of them passed forward a package of bread, hoarded from previous meals to help them survive the siege.

I accepted the bread. I had not said Mass for a group since before I came to Nikde. I was out of practice, and I did not have my book. But I could remember how to bless the bread. I led the men through several prayers and shared the Eucharist with them. As each man took the bread from my fingers, he walked to the door and raised his hands. The last two were the ones with the guns, which they set on the ground before me.

All that remained in the building was me, the unconscious leader of the rebellion, and two dead bodies. After a few minutes, Baader came through the door. He picked up the guns from the floor and unloaded them. We stood over Doctor Golc's body for several minutes.

"They are talking about a priest. You cannot stay here."

"I know."

We walked out of the building, and he led me to the hospital. I packed the small satchel I had arrived with, then joined Baader where he stood in the main ward. The two wounded soldiers had been treated by their fellows and were gone. We were alone. I turned to Baader.

"Bless me, Father, for I have sinned...."

I left when it was dark.

Part 3

Underground

1944

1

I left the mine at night. The road took me through Nikde, and I stopped in front of the clinic, where I knew Lida was still awake, reading, because of the candlelight from her window. I felt the pull of her, the attraction of the life I thought I had given up forever. Tempted, I even put my hand on the door; she would take me back if I asked her.

Then I stopped. Lida was part of a world I did not belong in anymore. I could not give up my vows. With my hand on the door, I prayed a blessing over Lida. I did love her. I knew then, if I saw her in fifty years, I'd recognize her smile.

I walked away from the clinic and out of the village.

I did not consciously choose to walk the forest paths. My only thought was to leave Nikde behind me, and the quickest route was into the trees. I knew if I followed the paths long enough, I would come across some woodcutters, those tough, earthy men who have done the same work, with the same tools, generation after generation since before Rome was founded.

I walked until it was too dark to see the path. I had some dark bread and a bit of cheese in my bag, but I did not feel like eating. Baader had given me a canteen on a belt before I left, and I contented my stomach with a little water.

In the morning, I woke up to myself. The man in Nikde faded into a memory, until even his name disappeared. That man would stay with Lida in my memory, but he was no longer me. I had my own identification papers, and no reason to think anyone could connect me to Lidice or Nikde. I practiced saying my name as I walked along.

I walked for several days. I approached any cabin I came across, and was welcomed every time. No one asked questions when I said I meant to cross the forest; they just shared their food and their shelter and wished me luck. I suspected some of them did not even know about the war.

I was deep in the forest, and looked like I'd been there for years when I found the boy. I had stopped at a stream to wash, and heard someone cry nearby as I waited for my clothes to dry. I put them on still wet and followed the sound.

The boy had curled himself between the roots of a forest giant. I approached him slowly, and made sure he saw and heard me before I got to him. He did not seem scared of me. Instead, he reached out his arms and called to me.

"Please help! My papa is hurt!"

I pulled him out of the depression between the roots and set him on his feet.

"Where is your papa?"

"He's back at the hut. He hurt his leg, and I couldn't help him."

"Can you take me to him?"

The boy grabbed my hand and pulled me into the forest. There was no path, but the way he ducked between trees instead of going around them made me think this was his private highway. These trees were his school and playground.

The hut he brought me to was small, but built with great care. The logs fit tight without mud, and looked like they would keep out any wind. The door was still open from the boy's departure, and he led me in without stopping.

"Papa? I brought help!"

I could smell the man's fever and sickness before I came though the door. The room was dim, lit only by what came through the door. At first I thought the man had left, until the pile of blankets in one corner rolled over with a groan. The boy ran to the figure and grabbed his hand.

"Papa? He's going to help you."

I knelt at the man's side and unwrapped the blankets he had twisted around himself. The layer closest to his skin was stiff with blood and piss. I pulled it all away and saw the sharp end of a branch. The skin around the wood was black and dead, and angry red streaks radiated up and down his leg. I pulled up the man's shirt. The lines continued past his groin and up his abdomen. I turned to the boy.

"When did this happen?"

"Two days ago. I was here, and he came in with that branch in his leg. He told me to go get help. But I couldn't find anybody.

When I came back, he yelled at me, but kept calling me the wrong name. I ran away because he hit me, but I don't think he meant to."

"No, he didn't. Your father is very sick, and he can't recognize you right now."

The boy burst into tears.

"Now, now, don't worry. He'll know you when he gets better, but I need your help right now. Can you help me? I need you to be big and strong."

"I'm strong."

"I knew you would be. Can you bring me some water? I need two buckets of clean water."

"I can do that. I can bring you three buckets if you need them."

"That's a good lad. And I need a kettle. Do you have one? Or a metal pot?"

The boy ran to the other side of the hut and pulled a battered kettle from a shelf.

"That's perfect. Now, you go fetch the water."

"Yes, sir. I'll go fast!"

The boy ran out the door, and I gave the man a closer examination. The branch was nearly as thick as my wrist, and went all the way through the man's thigh. The man was not conscious, but did keep moaning. I didn't know what I could do for him, but I had to try.

Next to the door was a box of kindling and a nearly depleted pile of wood. In the back of the hut was a crude stone fireplace full of cold ashes. I built a small fire, then looked for any tools I could use.

On the same shelf as the kettle sat an earthen jug. I pulled the stopper and was nearly bowled over by the smell of strong spirits. On the rough table, I found the man's pocketknife, the blade sharper and cleaner than any other instrument in the place.

By this time, I could hear the boy coming back. He struggled with the weight of the water bucket, so I went out to help him. He didn't come in with me when I picked up the bucket, but ran to the side of the hut and came back with another empty bucket and ran back into the trees.

Inside again, I poured some of the water into the kettle and hung it over the fire. I poured more into a cup and set it aside. I washed my hands, and used the rest to wash the wound as best I could. I did not think I could either push or pull the branch out of the wound, but I thought I could cut along the length of the branch and remove it that way. I was much more worried about the red lines of infection.

I thought back to my time in the hospital. Not long after I arrived, I witnessed a death by blood poisoning. The man died as his body simply burned itself away. He'd had the same red streaks along his skin.

The boy brought in the second bucket of water just as the kettle reached the boil. I put the knife into the boiling water, then used the second bucket to wash the man's leg of the rest of the gore. After a few minutes, I pulled the knife out and doused both it and the wound with the alcohol from the jug. Then I looked at the boy.

"I have to cut your father's leg to get the stick out. I think you should wait outside."

"You're going to cut my papa?"

"Yes, but it will make him better."

The boy studied my face for a long moment before he decided he could trust me with his father. He nodded and went outside.

I twisted myself around until I could see both ends of the branch. It was not deep under the skin. I touched the knife blade to the swollen skin, and it split at the slightest pressure. The man did not even move. I sliced the length of the branch, and the skin peeled back, away from the blade. I pulled on the branch, and the whole thing came out, followed by a gush of foul green pus. I had to turn to the side and vomit before I could continue. I poured the rest of the second bucket of water along the wound and washed out what I could. The blood that did come out was thick and dark, nearly a syrup. I poured the last of the alcohol over the wound. The man did not even flinch.

I didn't have anything to bind the wound with, but as long as it drained, I didn't want to cover it. I moved to the man's head and tried to pour a little water into his mouth. His lips were cracked and dry. He would not take any water. I felt for the large vessel in his neck.

There was nothing to feel. The man had died while I operated. The blood had come, not from his heart beating, but from the release of pressure of the branch.

I sat back on my heels for a long time, looking at the man. I did not want the boy to see the horror of my surgery, so I wrapped the man up in the cleanest of the blankets so only his face showed. I anointed his eyes, mouth, and hands with oil from my satchel before I washed the knife and my hands with the cooled water from the kettle and tossed the branch into the fire. I used the rest of the blankets to mop up the fluids from the floor, then rolled them together and carried them outside.

The boy was just outside the door. He looked at me as I came out.

"Papa?"

How could I tell him his father was dead?

"I'm so sorry."

"Papa?" He moved toward the door. I dropped the blankets and grabbed him.

"Don't, boy. Don't look."

The boy sagged against me and I held him as he wept. After a time, I thought he had settled himself down and I loosened my grip. As I let go of his shoulders, he turned into an enraged animal.

"You said you would help him! You said you would fix him!" He scratched my arms and tried to hit my face. I could not raise my hands to defend myself. I let him exhaust himself.

We did not go into the hut that night. I built a fire outside and only went in to find what little food they had inside. I tried to get the boy to eat, but he refused. I sat up and stared into the fire long after the boy fell asleep.

In the morning, I found a shovel among the tools set against the hut. I dug a grave while the boy tried to hammer two pieces of wood into a cross. I had to help him in the end, when he couldn't get the nails to go all the way in. Then I brought out the man and set him in the grave. Before I covered the body, I pulled out my stole and breviary and recited the funeral prayers. The boy had probably never been to a church, but he followed my movements and crossed himself when I did. We pushed the dirt in together, and I drove the simple Cross into the loose soil. I went once more into the hut to find any possessions the boy might need. There was not much. I found a spare shirt and a photograph of a young, pretty woman I could only imagine was the boy's mother. I added the father's knife to the bundle.

We walked through the forest all that day and camped down in the trees when it became too dark to see the trees. I tried to talk to the boy, but he would not speak. At night, he cried for an hour before he passed out, exhaustion and grief too much for his little body. I kept the fire going all night, so he would not wake to darkness.

I thought back through the last few days. I could not save the woodcutter; I didn't have the tools, medicines, knowledge or time. He was dead before I arrived at the hut, regardless of the beating of his heart or the flow of his blood. I could not save his body.

But his soul. His soul. For the first time since I came to Nikde, I felt like a real priest. I comforted someone in pain, and eased his passing; I cared for the survivors; I gave a situation I could not control into God's hands, and led with my heart instead of my head.

I looked at the sleeping boy. So young. I did not know how to care for a child, and I did not think he could travel with me. I needed to find a safe place for him, where he could become accustomed to his new life and grow into a man. I could not take care of his life, but I would do everything I could for his soul.

The boy stirred, then sat up. He stared into the fire for a long time, then came over and leaned against my shoulder. He did not cry. I don't think he could. I put my arm around him, and we waited for the sun to rise.

In the morning, we set off again. Near noon, we found a small village, and the boy's eyes lit up. He knew this place. He ran ahead of me, straight to the door of one of the houses. He knocked on the door, and a woman opened it for him. She looked very surprised, but quickly gathered the boy to her. I came up to her.

She was the woodcutter's sister, the boy's aunt. I explained what had happened, and showed her my stole as proof of my priesthood. She thanked me and invited me to stay in the village until the men could recover the woodcutter's body for a proper funeral. They did not have a church, but they did have a cemetery, and she wanted everything to be properly done for her brother. I agreed.

It took a few days for three men to maneuver a cart through the trees and return with the body. I spent that time with the villagers. They were cut off from the outside world, and had only a vague knowledge that there even was a war going on. They cared for each other, and for their land. They had almost nothing. But each house had a fire for warmth, food for the body, and a Bible. Enough of them knew how to read that they could share the Word and pray together.

They had such a simple, honest faith. I had never seen the like. When the rest of the village found out about my priesthood, I was asked to baptize every child under the age of six, which told me how long it had been since a priest had come this way.

The funeral of the woodcutter was simple. The cemetery was a clearing, surrounded by ancient trees. They did not have headstones, but the women fashioned a cross from woven grasses. We buried him as a community, and even I, a stranger, was a member. As we walked away from the cemetery to the meal, a feast everyone contributed what they could, I stopped and watched. This was what the Church was supposed to be. It made me think of the little church in Rome, tiny and crumbling in the middle of opulence.

These were the people, the real people, of the Church, of Faith. Their simplicity was holier than all the gold and jewels of the High Church.

We ate together. I knew the boy would grow here. He was safe and loved. He had his family. The next day, I picked up my satchel and the sack of leftover food from the feast. I thought about staying, but while I had found real Faith, I had not found my place in the world yet. But I was able to leave with a lightness I had not felt since before Lidice.

I wandered for the rest of that autumn, and spent the winter with a community of shepherds. In the spring, word came that the Russians had pushed the Germans out of the eastern part of Czechoslovakia. Many times, I met convoys of German soldiers; all headed northwest, their eyes locked on nothing. By the third time a group of trucks drove past me, I realized why the soldiers looked so odd to me: none of them carried guns.

I had seen a very small part of the war. Huge battles raged in other countries; I only read about them. But what I did see proved to me, anyone who fought against the Nazis, even if they were Communist, was a hero.

I came across many celebrations as I traveled. As a stranger, I was inundated with questions as soon as I came into a town: were the Russians really coming? What about the Americans? Did I know if Berlin had fallen? Each time, I tried to explain that I had less knowledge than they did, but few believed me.

I saw other signs of the end of the War. In one village, where I stopped for supplies, I could smell and see smoke, as well as what I thought was burning pork as I walked through empty streets. When I reached the center of town, I met a grisly sight: the townspeople stood around a burning house. I stopped at the edge and spoke to a man who held his young daughter in his arms.

"Whose house is this? Why aren't you all trying to put out the fire?"

He looked at me for a long time before he answered.

"Germans lived there."

He did not look at me again, and I left the village without asking for any food.

2

A man returned to childhood is a giant. For three years, I'd done my best not to think about home. Home belonged to the hidden me; the man in Nikde did not have a father or mother, a sister, friends, or even a life before Lidice. He never missed this place; only when I let him die did home become real.

I approached the town from the south, across newly planted wheat fields. I could smell home, the combination of old sheep and new bread. I saw the cross at the top of the church steeple that marked the center of town. I jumped a stone fence onto the road, and picked up a rock, a piece of home, and weighed it with my fingers. It felt good, solid. I slipped the rock into my pocket and walked into town.

I walked between the stone buildings; the whitewash had faded with time, and many roofs were missing tiles, but the people kept the streets swept. I walked through the streets until I stood in front of the church. I was not ready to go in, but I smiled as the memories came back: Midnight Mass, when every seat was filled; my first Lent as an altar boy; the day I stood in front of the congregation and announced my calling. The building had not changed, and I said a prayer as I stood before it that it never would.

The people, though, were changed. I did not recognize anyone, could not recognize anyone; faces were thin, clothes were tattered, children were hesitant in their play. The war had been over for months, but no one was quite ready to believe they had survived. The years made everyone a stranger.

I found the street where I had been born. We had lived at the end of the lane. Two new houses stood where an overgrown and unused hog lot had provided hours of childhood entertainment. The tree my sister, Ryba, had jumped out of to prove she could fly was gone. A new, short wooden fence surrounded the garden. Mother had wanted one for years, to keep out the neighbor's goat.

A small boy sat in the dirt in front of the house. He waved at me when I reached the gate, then gave a howl of delight as he threw twin handfuls of dirt into the air. I laughed with him as he showered his head with the tiny clods. I could remember his mother doing the same thing. The door to the house opened, and a woman came out.

The hair was shorter, the face was slimmer, but it was Ryba. She picked up the boy and dusted him off with a quick hand, and sent him on his way with a pat on his backside into the house. She walked toward the gate with squinted eyes.

"Can I help you?"

I tried to talk. The best I could manage was a toad imitation.

"Are you alright, sir?"

"Ryba…?"

"How do you…" She stopped. I didn't dare breathe. "Jan?"

I touched my face. In the months since I left Nikde, I had let my beard and hair grow. I looked down and saw my clothes from her point of view; dirty, torn, crudely patched. If I'd had a mirror, I wouldn't have recognized myself either.

I tried to open the gate to get in, but I could not work the latch. So I jumped it. Or, instead, I tried to jump it. My toe caught on the top board and I spilled onto the stone path. Ryba gave a yelp. I stood up, and she cried out.

"You're bleeding! Come here, your head is bleeding!"

She pulled a kerchief out of her sleeve and held it against my head. She grabbed my arm and pulled me through the front door.

Inside, the little boy was in Mother's lap, babbling out a story of great concern and few words. She laughed when he did, but stopped when we entered. I wanted to speak. I opened my mouth.

And Ryba, as she had since she could, spoke first.

"Mama! It's Jan! It's Jan!"

Mother had aged. Her hair, jet-black in my childhood, now with scattered strands of gray, was pulled back into the same bun she always wore. She stood with a cane she had not used when I left. I came to her and caught her when she tried to move faster than she could. She wept into my shoulder.

3

We sat. We talked. They told me their war stories. How Ryba had led a campaign against any group of German soldiers unlucky enough to pause for the night in the area. Not one armored car or troop truck survived the night without punctured tires and syphoned gasoline. One night of legend, she and her friends stole every pair of boots and shoes in a German camp. Thirty men had to march to the next town in bare feet.

Mother had kept her house, tended her garden and grandchildren, and kept an illegal radio and pistol in her root cellar. She still had the radio, but made Father turn the pistol in to the doddering old village constable as soon as she heard about the surrender.

The children multiplied the longer we talked. The oldest, a stretched out six year old version of Ryba, came back with Father. The two had been in the fields, hunting wild onions. The little boy from the front yard was the middle child. And a squawk from my old room introduced me to the youngest, another daughter, born the day I left Nikde.

Father had not changed. The eyes could still change from stone to ice to fire, and his moustache predicted the weather better than any almanac. He moved to shake my hand, but changed to a tight embrace. After a minute, he snuffled his nose into his handkerchief and gave me the sort of stern look his grandchildren would laugh at.

"And where have you been, boy? Your mother has been worried."

"I'm sorry, Father. I didn't want to worry anyone. I just couldn't come home."

"What happened out there?"

I didn't know how to tell what I had seen. How could I describe mounds of bodies afire, or men dying as I held their hand? How to tell them about the man I abandoned? They had been occupied, but the worst of the war passed the village. When I didn't answer, Father nodded to me. He'd been in the last war; he knew.

"It's alright. You'll tell us when you're ready. Are you here to stay?"

"I don't know. I haven't contacted the Bishop or the Church in years. I don't know where or what I am supposed to be."

Father clapped his hand on my shoulder.

"That is a worry for another day. Now is for celebration! Wife! We need wine!"

"It's in the pantry, Husband, and you can fetch it yourself if you are so in need of a drink."

An old act, to be sure. We had grown up with Father pretending to growl orders at Mother, and her telling him what she thought of those orders. They did not fight. Instead, they lived a life of quiet, and quite false, disrespect that kept the whole family laughing.

This was home. I had left. I hadn't left. I couldn't ever fully leave.

Father brought in a bottle of wine, dusty with time. He blew on it to clean it, and the label came off. I picked it up: *Chateau Chasse-Spleen* 1922.

"Been saving this. I knew you would come back someday. Thought we would want something to celebrate with. Lucky for us, nobody ever thought to dig through the entire pile of turnips."

Ryba brought four glasses from the kitchen and Father pried the cork from the neck. He filled our glasses and raised his in a toast, but struggled with the words for a moment.

"There should be some poetry for this, but I cannot think of any. So, simply, and purely, welcome home, Jan."

We drank and did the best we could to keep the horrified expressions off our faces. Knowing Father, this had started life as a dubious vintage, and six years under the turnip pile had not improved its character. The wine had somehow been infused with an overtone of feet. Father did not hide his reaction.

"I'm going to skin that damn trader!"

"Husband!"

"Vintage French wine, my goat's aunt!"

Mother tried not to laugh, but could not contain herself, which set Ryba and me to giggling, and finally Father joined us. Father could trade and barter with farmers all day long and come out ahead in the deal, but he had a weakness for things he considered luxuries. Mother's tight grip on the family purse strings usually kept Father's enthusiasm in check.

Mother and Father promised to watch over the children while Ryba and I went for a walk. She led me down the street, and we talked about our time as children in our little village. We passed the house where a tiny old woman, who died before I left for the Seminary, used to invite us in for pastries and a cool drink during the summer. She knew Father as a child, and told us many stories he did not want us to know. Further down the street, our old school still stood, empty in the evening. Ryba's oldest would start there in the next term. The hedge on the edge of the school property had been my favorite hiding place when I did not feel like playing with my schoolmates. It seemed so tiny, and I could not imagine how I managed to worm between the rows of prickly branches.

We made our way down to the shops. The sole tavern in the village had not reopened, but we were not the only ones out for a ramble. I did not recognize many of the people, but they knew Ryba. She explained how so many people had left the area, and their relatives took over their farms and shops.

The park near the church looked a bit worse for wear, but we found our old spot on the top rail of the fence.

"So. Where's your husband?"

"Out in the fields. He wanted to check on his family's property."

"I'm surprised he left the farm for the village."

"We thought the children would be safer here with Mother and Father. And I didn't want to leave them. Mother's leg never really healed. We couldn't get her to a doctor after the horse kicked her, and the bones did not set straight. Besides, I had much more fun here than I would have had digging turnips. And, after you left, Father needed help in the store. " The naughty grin came as quick as it had during our childhood.

She told me more of the schemes she had played on Germans, all of which seemed to end with embarrassed, and somewhat damaged soldiers. Her band of young women never killed anyone, but they did cause enough havoc to keep the district garrison busy.

"I suppose it was too much to expect you to take the war seriously."

"I did. I took it very seriously. But that is no reason not to have some fun."

We sat in silence.

4

5 July, 1945

Your Grace,

I am alive. I am sorry I did not have the courage to come back. I hope you will forgive me. I have wandered far and seen much, and I am not yet healed, but I am ready to become a servant of God again.

Jan.

6 July, 1945

My son,

You are a celebration. Come home as soon as you can. We need you here.

K.

5

I stayed with my family for a month. I needed the time to refresh my soul. I talked with Father and Mother, and met my nieces and nephew. The oldest girl read stories to me, while the youngest decided I was a comfortable bed. For the boy, I was the world's greatest toy: one part pony, two parts portable tree to climb. I could not help but spoil all three.

I had never longed to have children. While my school friends married and started families, I was praying over dying miners. And I did not regret my choice. But I did see the joy of children, of parenthood. While the three could conspire to create more noise than I thought possible, it was always happy noise. It was life. It was continuation. When I saw the three of them, finally asleep and quiet at the end of a day of triumphs and tragedies, the time I spent away disappeared.

The nightmares did not disappear.

Not every night, but often enough, I saw dead men. Father told me Lidice was not the only massacre, and definitely not the last horror. He showed me newspapers he had kept throughout the war. Days after Lidice, another village, Ležáky, received the same treatment by the Germans. They did not try to hide or justify their actions. Instead, the Nazi propagandists glorified the mass killings. The papers even had photographs of the dead. Hundreds of men dead, the women and children disappeared into Poland.

The piles stayed in my mind. Arms and legs, bodies. Bullet holes. But no faces. The only faces I saw belonged to men who avoided the piles: the Rabbi; the Doctor. They still had eyes. They watched me.

I told Father about my dreams. He was a combat veteran.

"They won't ever stop completely. All you can hope is that they will someday sleep. I still see the men we left. They don't speak to me. They just stare at me, jealous of my breath."

"How do you live with them?"

"You remember that you did not kill them. They can't hurt you. They can only haunt you. There are so many ghosts now. Yours sound like good men."

"What about the men in the piles."

"They aren't haunting you. You're haunting them. It is time for you to let them rest. Don't forget them, and don't forget what you saw. But you aren't doing them or yourself any good by holding

them in their moment of death."

"I can't leave them!"

"You aren't leaving them. You're letting them go."

"I will try."

Father only sometimes played the fool.

6

The train to Brno ran full. People wanted to get home, get away, get somewhere new, find some place without memories. I had seen joy on the roads and town, but the train was silent.

I sat next to a woman only a few years older than me. Her son, no older than Ryba's oldest, had the window seat. He had a new toy train engine in his lap, but he did not play with it. His mother tried to interest him a few times in the toy. She made the right sounds, and moved it around. But the boy had forgotten how to play. He stared out the window, silent.

She finally gave up on the train. I did not want to intrude, but I could see the tears cut through her face powder. She was well-dressed, and wore one glove, the other removed and on her lap.

"Is your son alright?"

She did not answer for several minutes. I opened my satchel and showed her my stole and Breviary. She looked up into my eyes and I smiled at her.

"I'm a priest. And I promise you, anything you say will go no further than me."

She looked me in the eye before she nodded and looked at her hands.

"He's not my son. He is not anybody's son anymore." Her Czech was lined with German. She took a deep, shuddering breath, her face lined. She aged while I waited.

"He's not my son. He's my nephew. His mother was my sister. His father…"

She looked around, wary of any ears. I prompted her.

"His father?"

"His father was a German officer."

It clicked in my mind, but I wanted to be sure.

"Where are his parents?"

"They're dead. His father was a procurement officer, in charge of finding food. He stole it, mostly. He did not get orders to leave his post, so he stayed. The people…"

She closed her eyes.

"The people came for him. I was visiting. Wolfie and I were out for a walk when they came. He loved to see the cows in the field. We came back. The people had hung them, naked, from the tree in front of the house. I couldn't hide them from Wolfie. He saw them, swaying there. He used to climb that tree. He showed me how high he could go, just the night before.

"I couldn't even cut them down. I didn't dare go into the house. I had my purse, and my money for a ticket home. I pretended he was my son, and that he was deaf. The stationmaster took pity on us; let us on with one ticket."

They stayed on the train when I left at Brno. The boy did not make a sound.

7

As I made my way to the Cathedral, I walked down the streets where I had followed the Bishop. I paused at the fountain where we had seen the children. There were still children, possibly the same ones. But these children laughed. They kicked a homemade football to me, and I sent it lightly back. Their laughter went far to erase horror.

I did not go into the Cathedral. I was coming home, and home was not among the chairs and statues. Instead, I went around to the service door of the refectory, where, as a student, I had spent hours unloading sacks of food for the kitchen, barely a lifetime ago. The door was closed, not by a lock but by a warp in the frame that defeated anyone who did not know the secret. I twisted the handle, pushed, kicked the bottom, and gave a sharp tug. The door opened with a creak.

I scared an altar boy as I walked the halls. Nobody came down to the back entrance unless they were supposed to be there, and strangers were rare and escorted. He yelped, and then tried to act gruff. He deepened his voice, squared his narrow shoulders, and demanded why I was breaking into the building. I did my best not to laugh at him. I explained the Bishop expected me, and would he be so kind as to escort me.

The boy led me through bare halls that once held tapestries and paintings. As we neared the Bishop's office, the boy pointed it out, then hurried back down the hall. The door was open, and I could hear the Bishop as he talked to someone, but I could not hear any reply. I waited outside until two men, boys really, came out, heads down and ears red. They wore the white shirts and black pants I wore years ago, and I realized he had reopened the Seminary. I could not help myself as I came in the door.

"Your Grace, the Latin brother says I am to present myself for punishment. I failed the conjugation exam. Again."

He did not look up from the papers on his desk.

"You are going to have to do better, son. Latin is the language of our Mother Church, and we must follow the Rules of …"

I stepped further into the room. Maybe it was because I was dressed in torn and patched country clothes, or maybe he heard something in my voice, but he raised his eyes and saw my grin.

"Jan . . ."

I came closer to his desk. He abandoned dignity and ran around the desk to grab me in a hug. He cried the tears of a father.

He had changed during the three years I'd been gone. He'd seemed such an imposing figure during my Seminary days. Not just because of his position, but he was such a man of energy and health. He had always looked neat and organized, hair always trimmed, clothes always pressed. The man before me had aged, but he still held the same energy. Only now, there was a fanatical flame in his eyes. He had let his hair and beard grow during my absence, and he looked more like a mad mystic than the Church Father I had left behind.

After several minutes, he let go and held my shoulders at arms length. He tried to start talking several times, and had to clear his throat and blow his nose before he could get anything out.

"Where . . . how . . . where have you been, boy? I sent for you a month ago!"

"I wanted to come, sir, but my mother seemed to think I should spend some time with family. I tried to explain to her, but she's stubborn."

"There was a good reason you spent so much time polishing the floors of your dormitory, wasn't there? Why didn't you send word you would be coming today?"

"I honestly didn't think of it."

"No matter. You're here now. You're here."

He gestured to his visitor chair.

"Sit. We have much to discuss."

8

The sun slanted low through the windows as we talked. I told him my story. He blessed me as my Confessor. As night came, he brought out a green bottle covered in English, and a pair of glasses. He poured us each a drink of an amber liquid. I tried mine and nearly choked on too large a mouthful.

"Irish Whiskey. A gift from a grateful American reporter who sheltered with us for a time."

"Not quite like home, but good enough, sir. What has happened here? I've been gone so long."

"We survived. We helped. We failed sometimes. I'm a bit out of favor with Rome right now."

He refilled his glass and drank all of it at once.

"About the same time you left an order came down from Pius: remain neutral. We were supposed to provide help, but not take sides. I don't know if he feared Mussolini's anger, or if he thought we could stand on both sides."

He gave a bark of laughter.

"They even threatened to excommunicate me for bending their rules by hiding people. I'm not completely sure why they didn't go ahead with it. I guess I have some friends that made the Nuncio pause."

"Neutral? How could anyone remain neutral?"

"And you haven't heard the worst of it. We lost thousands of priests and monks in Poland. Thousands! And even then, Pius wanted to stay out of it.

"We're not hermits here! We live in the world, we work in the world, and without the people we are nothing. Nothing! As if I would defend an empty church."

"How many did we lose here, sir?"

He bowed his head.

"I don't know. I simply don't know. So many disappeared. You remember my file? I could not keep up with the reports. I don't know who is dead, who is missing, who is even still in the country. I have more empty churches than I can ever think to fill."

"What about the boys you had in here? How long until you have new priests?"

"We've only been open for a few months, and I hardly have anyone to teach them."

"You don't want me to teach Latin, do you?"

"I have not sinned nearly enough for that penance, my son. But I do think we can find something for you to do. If you're willing."

"I am still a priest, Your Grace. I go where my Bishop sends me."

"Well, for tonight, your bishop is sending you to the bathhouse and then to bed. And tomorrow, we will do what we can to make you look like a priest."

I stood and reached out to shake his hand. He grasped mine firmly and smiled with tears in his eyes.

"Welcome home, Father Jan."

9

All the years I had been away, I dreamed of my own parish. I wanted a place where I could meet people and preach the Word, where I could baptize babies and hear Confession, and teach Confirmation candidates. I wanted to argue with the parish women over how to decorate and wrestle with those whose faith had faltered.

The Bishop gave me all that, several times over. Because of the war, we had more parishes than priests, and everyone had to split their time among many churches. I slept at the Cathedral rectory, but every day saw me in a different corner of Brno, if not in a church then in a hospital or parishioner's home.

My favorite was a tiny church on the edge of town, where most of the church members were older than my parents. These were Catholics from another age: the women would not consider Mass without a veil and breakfast was not an option until after the service. I could not be there every morning, but at least four days each week, I began my day in that tiny, neat church, or I had better have a good excuse ready.

Within a month of my return, I performed my first wedding in my favorite church. The bride and groom were both from old neighborhood families, and I thought this would be the perfect opportunity to bring the parish fully back to life. I threw myself into the plans with gusto. I wrote and rewrote my homily, trying to find just the right story to tell, to make the day perfect for the couple and the community. I ransacked the few books left in the Seminary library, asked every priest what they thought I should say, and even wrote Ryba for advice.

The morning of the wedding, I was at the church before the sun rose. The groom's aunt had cleaned and ironed my robes, and I'd made a special visit to the barber the evening before. I fretted over the details of the altar. When the bride's family arrived, I tried to help, but it was soon apparent I was more a hindrance than help, and the bride's mother suggested I wait across the street in a café until they needed me.

When the time came, I stood at the altar and watched these two people, so young, come down the aisle. The groom was tall and thin, his suit too wide and too short for his frame. His forehead was beaded with sweat, though the church itself was slightly cool. I shook his hand, and noticed it trembled.

The bride was tiny, not even up to her soon-to-be husband's shoulder. Her dress was a simple white gown, with just a little lace. Her veil looked like it had gone down more than a few aisles. She blushed as she stood by the groom's side.

I started the Mass, and led the congregation through the prayers and blessings. Then came the time for me to speak. I stood, ready to recite the homily I had prepared when I realized I could not do so. Instead, I spoke from my heart.

"I had a homily prepared. But you two deserve something more than an essay on the Sacrament. Instead, I want to tell you a story. Obviously, I have little experience with married life, but I have seen many marriages that stood when they could have collapsed.

"These last few years, I travelled across our country quite a bit. Early on in my travels, I met an old farm couple. Their children had grown and left home, their fields were more than they could work. I split some wood for them to try to pay them back for their hospitality. They didn't have much, but they were willing to share.

"The day I spent with them, evil came in and tried to destroy them. Everything they owned, everything they worked for was destroyed in a moment, for no reason. They could have collapsed; they could have given up. They could have run away. But they didn't.

"Instead, they stood together. Instead of despair, they talked about the future; instead of mourning, they planned how to make things better than they'd been; instead of complaining, they held on to hope.

"It wasn't easy for them. There were tears and sadness, anger and regret. But the life they had together kept them strong.

"Life is not easy. But together, you are stronger than you were alone. Cling to each other. Don't just love when life is easy."

It was not a long talk. But it felt better in my heart than any of the drafts I had written and discarded.

The rest of the wedding proceeded, and soon the new couple and their families left the church to celebrate. I was invited to join them, but did not. They did not need me for this part of the celebration. I packed everything away, cleaned my part of the church, and returned home.

I had three peaceful years at the Cathedral, before new troubles started.

10

The Bishop called me into his office. We had gathered the day before to listen to President Beneš's speech as he stepped down from office and, without saying as much, turned the government over to the Communists. As soon as the speech ended, the Bishop locked himself in his office. He did not come out for the evening meal, and if he left during the night, nobody had been awake to see him.

It was early when the Seminarian woke me, and the sun barely breached the horizon as I knocked on the Bishop's door. His eyes answered my question about his sleep as he invited me in and sat me down.

I watched him pace. Over the years, I learned the Bishop could not think and be still at the same time.

"What do you know about Communists?"

I thought for a few minutes.

"Not much, really. I know they like to talk about making everyone equal. I know they don't like religion."

"It's more than that: Communism insists on atheism. To them, religion is rebellion, because it puts something higher than the state."

"I remember Father Josef talking about Karl Marx, and how the Russians were corrupting his ideas."

"He would have known better than I. They call themselves Communists, whatever they really are."

Back and forth, window to Crucifix; the carpet behind his desk was several shades lighter than anywhere else in the room.

"This is very hard for me, Jan. I don't want to ask you, but I don't have much choice."

"Ask me what?"

"I think the Communist parties are going to take over the whole government before too long. Beneš kept them from taking too much. Now…"

"Now he's gone."

"And nobody else has enough power to keep them in check. And you're right about one thing: they do not like us. God has no place in the Communist World. In Russia, there have been …

excessive reactions to Religion. Most of the Russian Orthodox leadership is either in exile in Western Europe or deep in Siberia."

"And you're afraid the same will happen here?"

"Very. We haven't recovered our losses yet, and Seminary classes are miniscule. We don't have enough bodies to meet the needs of our people. We lost a generation of priests."

"You don't think they would try to send us to prison, do you?"

"Not quite. But my brother Bishop in Prague has people on the inside of various government offices. There is a draft resolution going around the departments, the Communist controlled departments. One of his people stole a copy, and he sent it to me."

He pulled a sheet of paper from his desk and passed it over to me. It had the look of an official document.

Roman Catholic clergy are to cease daily observances and celebrations. Priests and Bishops are to limit their activities to one (1) ritual per church or cathedral on Sundays. Funerals are permitted with proper government permission (see attached forms) within three (3) days of death. After that point, secular authorities will handle the funeral. Weddings are limited to secular authorities, under the Social Ministry.

Failure to comply with these edicts will result in arrest and imprisonment. Direct any inquiries to the local Social Ministry representative.

"I don't understand. Why cut down on how often we can say Mass?"

"The outright attacks on the clergy in Russia turned much of the population against the government. I assume they don't want a repeat here. Instead of making us illegal, they want to make us invisible and hope the people won't notice we're gone."

"I'm guessing you have come up with some options."

"I have. In times of great need and great danger, certain rules can be … stretched. And if we cannot bring the people into the Church, we will bring the Church to the people."

"What rules would those be?"

"We are going to need a different sort of priest. When the people see a man with a Roman collar, they know who he is. But what if he isn't wearing a collar? What if he isn't in a church? What if he looks like everyone else?"

"Nobody would notice him."

"Exactly. We have to assume the government has, or will have very soon, dossiers on every active priest in Czechoslovakia. So, we need priests who will not show up on any official list; priests who can blend in with the population. Priests who no one would ever suspect."

"This sounds very familiar."

"It should. You gave me the idea; you and your Major Baader. You both hid in the open and did the work, although it sounds like he was a bit better at hiding than you were."

I chose to ignore that.

"So, where are you going to find these priests who can hide in the open?"

"We're not going to be able to train them much. I need dedication and loyalty more than theology and philosophy. The perfect man is someone who wanted to be a priest, but couldn't for some reason or another. Like your classmates who couldn't come back during the war."

"Surely they've all made new lives for themselves by now."

"You're probably right. Which is why I want them. They already know how to blend in with the population."

"What if they're married? What if they have children?"

"All the better. Who would suspect a married father of being a priest?"

"This is insane! Are you going to ordain women, too?"

"Who knows? As I said, in extreme circumstances, rules can be stretched."

"This isn't stretching. This is cutting a cord and burning both ends!"

"Hardly. This is doing what has to be done, which I have always believed is part of my job."

"Do we have permission to do this?"

"I have no idea. I didn't bother asking. But we aren't the only ones. Don't worry so much. By the time anyone figures out what we've done, there will be little they can do about it."

I was not sure if his manic grin or the joy in his eyes when he spoke of breaking rules worried me more.

11

The Bishop gave me the details as I prepared for my new job. I wasn't supposed to do anything more than find the men and broach the subject. I'd explain the Bishop's idea, ask them to think about it, and move on to the next. I still wasn't comfortable with the whole idea, but it made sense, and I could not argue with the Bishop's logic. I tried, but it did me no good.

The day I left, the Bishop told me he had a present for me, something to help me on my mission. He led me to the old carriage house behind the parsonage, where the gardener kept fertilizer and hedge trimmers in happier days.

Cobwebs and dust created feeble light through the side window, and both of us coughed as the door stirred up a decade's worth of grit. In the middle of the open space, something was covered in a somewhat cleaner tarp. It had a very familiar shape.

"Impossible."

The Bishop gave me the smile he saved for those occasions when he knew he had gotten the better of someone.

"No, just merely improbable."

I pulled the tarp off and threw it aside. Underneath, cleaner than the last time I saw it, was the motorcycle I had abandoned in Lidice.

"How is this even possible?"

"When you didn't come back, I sent your friend Vavrinec to look for you. Well, 'sent' is not quite the right word. I didn't have time to send him. Anyway, he heard about the massacre and went to look around there. He found this where you left it, recognized it, and brought it back."

"Why didn't you tell me before?"

"To be perfectly honest, I forgot it was here. I only remembered when we started talking about you going underground again. I had it cleaned and tuned up last month."

I climbed onto the saddle and grabbed the handles. The leather on the seat was new, but the rest was the same. I rubbed my thumb along a knick in the leather of the right grip, the edge worn smooth from the habit. I turned on the engine and kicked it to life.

The roar was the same.

I sat for several minutes, eyes closed. I hadn't ridden since Lidice, but everything felt right. When I opened my eyes, the Bishop had his hands folded in prayer. As he finished, he pulled out a small glass bottle and blessed the motorcycle and myself with Holy Water.

I bowed my own head and prayed for guidance and strength.

And that night, I left in search of the first of my hidden priests.

12

I decided to start simple. My old classmates, Miklos, lived in Znojmo to the southeast of Brno. He had left Seminary during our final year to care for his father. I hadn't heard from him since, but I remembered his father had owned an art gallery. With that information, I knew I could find Miklos.

I arrived in the middle of a market day. I hid my motorcycle in an old barn on the edge of town and walked the rest of the way. I didn't carry anything with me to identify myself as a priest. My hope lay in recognition.

The women of the town knew the market, and knew how to remove someone who dared move too slowly while in their way. I made the mistake of pausing in front of a stand of onions. Before I even had the option to move, I felt something hit the back of my legs. I turned to see what had hit me, and an old woman who barely came up to my elbow shouldered her way past me with a grunt meant to reprimand me. In her hand was a cane she did not seem to need for walking.

I abandoned the battlefield and found a café, well stocked with husbands, their feet surrounded by baskets and canvas bags full of purchases they were to guard. Several of them had pushed two square tables together to play a game of double-deck pinochle. Players changed in and out of the game as their wives came to collect them. I bought a coffee at the bar and waited off to the side.

Eventually, a spot opened and the men looked for a new player. One old man, his cheeks unshaved of sparse grey whiskers, waved me over.

"Sit. Play."

I sat and looked at the hand the previous man abandoned: nines, Jacks, Queens, and a lonely looking Ace of Diamonds. The man next to me told me the trump was Hearts. I laughed at my hand. I could neither help nor hinder either side.

We played out the hand. My ace held for one hand, but I could do nothing with anything else and my team went set. As no one bothered to keep score in this shifting game, the pain of defeat lasted only a moment.

A quick flurry of wives decimated the players, and the next game required only one deck of cards. I partnered with the old man who invited me. Other than bids, he spoke only in grunts. He held up his cup, and a teenage waitress refilled him from a glass bottle of dark crimson liquid. He took a long drink and shuddered with pleasure. When I raised my eyebrows, one of the other men told me it was a wild cherry brandy the owner brewed in the back of the café for locals.

The game continued, and I studied the players. The man to my left wore stained and patched pants, and his shoes were caked with a thick layer of dried manure. His fingers were thick; he had trouble picking up individual cards. I didn't imagine he would be able to direct me anywhere in town.

The man to my right wore a suit more suited for a city office, although his tie peeked out of his breast pocket. He was a better bet as an informant, but kept his eyes on the door, as if he knew he would leave soon. As the game ended, an equally well dressed, although much plumper woman entered and beckoned him. He settled his hat on his head and followed her out without so much as a nod to the rest of us.

The old man gestured to the café owner to take the empty chair, but he shook his head and went back to wiping glasses. So, we played three-man pinochle. And I couldn't help myself. With the larger group, I had played like someone who knew the rules but hadn't played for a long time. I made myself into a safe player, able to support my side, but never making any great plays. But the game shifted to every man for himself, and I decided to have a bit of fun, since I wasn't in any particular hurry.

The two men knew each other. I figured that much about them from the start. And as I dealt the first hand, I could see them eye each other. I knew what would come next. They would play each other, and my role was to be that of a placeholder, someone who was there to throw in inconsequential cards, and provide neither with an edge. And if I played as I did in the four and eight player games that is all I could do.

But I'd learned the game from my grandfather, who paid for my father's education and started a business with his winnings.

As the game progressed, I read the men. Each knew how to play, but neither knew how to control the cards. Within two rounds of each deal, I knew their hands better than they did. I played them against each other: I didn't take the bid, and I only took enough hands to keep my meld. Instead of playing to win, I played to make them lose. Whoever took the bid would find himself against an opponent who, somehow, kept getting fed just enough points to go set. My score crept up slowly, while each of the others plummeted into deep negative scores. By the end, my score of two hundred points won easily. Before we could start another game, his wife pulled the farmer away from the table.

The old man refilled his cup, and gestured for me to have a drink with him. I accepted and sipped the sweet alcohol.

"Very clever. Didn't think you had that in you, stranger."

The words sounded like a shoe drug through gravel.

"What do you mean?"

"Don't play dumb. You think I've never seen anyone pull that before? I've done it myself. Never worked more than twice in the same place, though. So, who taught you to play?"

"My grandfather. He picked up the game when he was young."

"He must have been one hell of a player."

"He did alright."

His chuckle wasn't any smoother than his words.

"I imagine he did. So, where are you from? I know all the decent players around here, and you aren't either of them."

I didn't want to give too much truth to a stranger.

"Nikde. Out in the mountains."

"Little place, right? Coal mines?"

"That's right. I think we were the only family in town without anyone down in the hole."

"Did a bit of that, long time ago. Didn't last long. Like the sunshine too much."

He finished his drink. It didn't seem to bother him much, but I decided to sip mine slow. The drink was strong and sneaky.

"What brings you here?"

"Just passing through. Thought I could get something to eat."

"Lots of people passing through these last few years."

"Everyone looking for a new home."

"You looking for a new home?"

"No, I'm looking for something else. Do you know if there is an art gallery anywhere around here?"

"Art gallery?"

"Yeah. When I got to town, I remembered my sister's birthday is next month. She wants to be an artist. Since I'm here, I thought I would look around."

"Well, there used to be one, just down the street. But it closed during the War. Damn Germans took everything."

"That's too bad."

"You might want to talk to the owner. Actually, it's the owner's son. He's wanted to reopen, but nobody's been painting much lately. Maybe your sister could show her stuff there."

"That's possible. Do you know where I can find him?"

"He should be at the hotel across the road here, behind the desk. Just ask for Miklos."

13

The hotel lobby was decorated in faded pink and cream striped wallpaper, and the front desk stood in front of an empty wooden frame, where only a corner of mirror remained. Nobody stood behind the desk, but when I rang the bell, a voice came from the next room.

"I'll be with you in a moment. Just need to finish with this tea."

The man who bustled in only vaguely resembled the boy I had known. Glasses, a new decoration, narrowed his already beak-like nose, and his hairline crept steadily towards the midway point between nose and nape.

"How may I help you?"

He did not recognize me. I wondered how much I had changed. How did I wear my years? I looked in the corner of mirror that remained and did not see the man Miklos would recognize. My skin remained unscarred, but my eyes were older and hooded. My forehead wrinkled where smooth skin once sat. The hairs of my weeklong beard held far more grey than my father's had when I was a child. I could pass for a decade older than my age.

I turned away from the mirror to find Miklos's eyes on my face. His face held concern, and I wondered how long I had stared into the mirror.

"Are you alright, sir?"

Sir. Was I old enough to be a sir? Thoughts for another day.

"Yes, I'm fine Miklos."

"How do you know my name?"

Miklos left Seminary months before Father Josef died, but he'd known the old man well. I'd spent much of the ride in thought of how to connect to the men I searched for.

"Father Josef always did call you slow."

His eyes narrowed.

"Father Josef … who are …"

I smiled at him.

"Jan? My God, Jan? Is that you?"

I held out my hand, but he grabbed me in a hug.

"What are you doing here? Can you stay long? Are you still in Seminary? Do you need a room? Do you want a drink?"

"Slow down, my friend. Do you have someplace we can talk? Someplace we won't be interrupted?"

"What's going on, Jan?"

"Please. We need to talk, and I need what I say to remain private."

We locked eyes for several minutes before he nodded.

"Alright. But not right now. I have to stay here and be available for guests. Do you want a room?"

"Thank you, but no. I'll have to leave as soon as we're done with our talk."

He grabbed a key from the pegboard to the side of the desk.

"Take this and go upstairs. We live on the top floor. I'll come take you up when I can. We'll talk then."

I saw the ring on his finger and did not ask questions.

14

I spent the hours in my room with a book I found in the hotel lobby. At noon, a teenage girl left a tray of bread and cheese to my door. I caught a glimpse of her as she walked back down the hall.

My surroundings did not inspire me much. The war had ended four years before, but without guests, the hotel could not recover. Hints of elegance remained in the fragments of gold paint on the lamps, and the moth-eaten bedclothes showed signs of a more prosperous history. But a bullet hole directly over the head of the bed gave the room a haunted feel, and I did not envy anyone forced to stay.

I kept the lamps off until the room darkened beyond my ability to read. I lit one, an old-fashioned oil lamp without enough oil to last the night, and waited. I dozed until I heard a soft tap on my door and a key in the lock.

Miklos peeked his head around the door, then came in and shut the door behind him. He kept one hand on the door and gestured for me to blow out the lamp and follow him. We crept down the hallway, past the lift-less lift shaft, through a door to what turned out to be a set of servant stairs. He led me to the top, and we went through a low door at the top.

"This used to be the servants quarters. The owner said we could live up here. He doesn't trust the night clerk, so I'm supposed to check up on him a few times each night. He's usually asleep, but we're not exactly booming with business, so it hasn't mattered yet."

There wasn't a hallway behind the door. Instead, we entered a low-ceilinged, well-lit room. A tiny woman hurried between table and kitchen. As Miklos entered, her face brightened, and she set the steaming pot on the table, then ran over to embrace him.

"Jan, this is my wife: Ana."

I held out my hand.

"I'm so happy to meet you."

"Miklos told me he was bringing an old school friend up for dinner. I hope you like Rajská."

"Ana makes the best Rajská Omacka in town."

I sniffed at the air and smiled. I could smell the beef, a rare enough pleasure, and the tomatoes, peppers, onions, and vinegar. Mother always made the dish for Father's birthday.

"I'm sure it will be wonderful."

She gestured to the table.

"Sit. I just about have everything ready."

Miklos led me to the table and pulled out a chair for me. When I sat, he ducked into the kitchen and brought out two glasses of cloudy beer and sat one of them in front of me. Ana came in with a glass of milk and sat. She took the lid off the dish in the middle of the table and slid in a spoon.

Miklos reached for the spoon, then glanced at me. I had folded my hands over my plate and lowered my head. He drew his hand back and copied my movements. I peeked out and saw Ana give me a small grin at her husband's expense.

I blessed the food, the home, and my hosts. And then I grabbed my fork and looked expectantly at the dishes, which brought a laugh from the couple. Ana took a knife to the narrow loaf of bread and put several slices on each place. Miklos dug the spoon into the dish and put a generous portion of Rajská over the bread.

"So. What is it you wanted to talk about?"

I looked at Ana. Miklos followed my glance and shook his head.

"She stays. Whatever you have to say to me, you will say in front of her."

"Alright. But first, I have to ask you something."

"Go ahead."

"Do you regret leaving Seminary? You always had such fire for the priesthood."

Miklos sat back in his chair, his fork in hand. A drop of sauce fell on his trousers, but he didn't notice. He sighed and reached for Ana's hand.

"Sometimes, I do. But I found so much more out here in the world than I think I could have found if I stayed. Ana and I were neighbors as children. When Father became sick, she came over everyday to check on us. She cooked and made sure I cleaned the house. When he slept, we talked. And, before too long, I couldn't stand a day unless I saw her. After Father died, I thought about returning to Brno. When I heard the Germans closed the Seminary, I decided it was a sign God had other plans for me. And, I simply did not want to go back. Ana showed me a different life, and I love it. I love her."

I watched both their faces as he talked, and I nodded as he finished.

"You made the right choice. I can see you two belong together. And I'm not surprised by your answer. But I think you might be surprised by my next question. What if you could still be a priest?"

"I'm married, Jan. Or did you not see the ring?"

"I saw it. Just answer the question. If you could, would you still want to be a priest?"

"I know I left early, but I also know the rules. And the rules say 'no married priests.'"

"What if things weren't so set in stone?"

"So, you want to know if I would leave Ana and go back to Seminary?"

"No, on both counts. You would stay married and be a priest."

"Well, since we can only be speaking hypothetically, then, yes, I would do that. As long as I can stay with Ana. We just got some wonderful news from the doctor last week, and she, they, come first in my life."

I looked at Ana, and she put a protective hand on her flat stomach. I could not help but grin.

"Well, congratulations to both of you. And I'm not speaking hypothetically. I'm here to ask you to take up your path to priesthood again."

I explained the Bishop's idea of secret priests, hidden among the population, serving the people as best they could. By the time I finished, the two of them held hands over their plates of uneaten food. I did not want the meal to go to waste, so I ate while I talked.

"You don't have to answer me right now. Think about it. Talk about it. You're just the first person on my list, so you have some time to play with. If you want to do this, come to the Cathedral on the first of September. I have to tell you, there may be some danger for both of you, all three of you, if you say yes. But if you don't want to do this, stay home. All I ask is keep this within these walls. Don't tell anyone who I am, or that I was even here."

"Of course. This is a bit of a shock. I thought I had made my choice. And it was a tough one, let me tell you. I told you why I didn't come back. I didn't tell you how close I came to leaving Ana. I had my bag packed, and was actually on the station platform, ticket in hand. I'm so happy I stayed, but it was a very near thing. And now, I have the chance to have both?"

"As I said, don't decide now. Think it over."

We finished the rest of the meal in more pleasant conversation. I told stories of our time in Seminary together, including a few Ana loved, but Miklos, I thought, did not enjoy so much. We laughed over the Palačinky, and Miklos tried to talk me into staying the night with the promise of more beer. But I could not.

The moon was high as I made my way back to my motorcycle. I had a long night ride ahead of me.

15

I moved from man to man, place to place. Some of the men I rejected after a quick observation, not even meeting them. Others, I pretended I just happened to be in the area and stopped on impulse. Some no longer lived where I remembered.

Three of them were dead.

But the few I broached the subject with, the ones I thought could live with the choice, listened. I promised nothing, and asked them to do the same. I left them with a date to come to the Cathedral if they wanted to join us.

I returned to Brno in time to see the threatened restrictions put into action. With the reduced number of public services, I had a large amount of free time to fill. I spent much of it learning the art of forgery. I learned to alter identification papers and passports, and searched through obituary archives to find identity candidates. With the war, so many people had simply disappeared, and I was able to create an impressive file of nearly finished paperwork in need of a final signature and photograph. My forgeries were not perfect, but they would stand up to a casual look.

Inside the Cathedral, life changed. As we could only say Mass on Sunday mornings, the Bishop took that job on his own shoulders, and spread the rest of the priests out through the city. I lived in the Bishop's residence, but spent my Sundays with my favorite parish, although time was taking a hard toll on the elderly members. Every month brought a funeral or two.

Despite all edicts, the Cathedral doors were kept open to anyone who needed sanctuary and comfort. They did not come through the main doors, but we developed a system that kept everyone busy. Daily Confessions moved to the old rose garden at the Seminary, where two benches were moved to sit on either side of a narrow hedge. A priest in civilian clothes sat on one, a newspaper open in his hands; the penitent would sit on the other bench with a book or a bit of knitting to occupy their hands while they spoke through the leaves.

September brought seven of the men I recruited. I met them in our old dormitory, closed and thickly webbed from disuse. We kept our reunion quiet, and I gave them the plan to sneak into the Cathedral. Like the schoolboys we had been, they knew all the quiet, almost secret routes in and out of the places we weren't supposed to go, including the Cathedral, a tradition passed to each group of first-year seminarians. The brothers knew, and most had done the same in their time, which did nothing to curb their ire for any boy unlucky enough to take a wrong turn. This time, without the punishment of floor scrubbing and extra Latin looming, some of the fun disappeared.

They waited in the Seminary until midnight, while I returned to help the Bishop prepare. We could not use the Cathedral proper for our activities, so we created our own church in the cellar. A table became our altar, and a simple silver Crucifix stood against the back wall. We left the dirt floor. It felt right.

I met the men at the top of the stairs and led them down. They stayed silent as we come into the candlelight, and each came forward to clasp the Bishop's hand as he greeted them by name. I stood near the wall as the rest moved into a circle around the Bishop.

"Thank you all for coming. I know this was a hard decision for you. It is not easy for me to do this. As a Church, we are held together with our traditions. I would prefer you to finish your education, become Deacons, train in a parish, and fulfill the qualifications for ordination. This is not possible. You must be hidden from the start."

The Bishop looked each man in the eye as he spoke.

"If any of you do not want to travel down this path, I must ask you to leave and forget you were ever here. I will bear you no grudge, and will continue to think of you as a brave and true son of the Church."

None of the men moved.

"Very well. Then it is time for you to make your oath to the Church."

He placed a large Bible on the altar. One at a time, the men came forward and swore to obey the teachings and rules of the Church, her bishops, and to remain silent and secret about their vocation. As the last stepped back, the Bishop led us all in prayer for all priests. When he lifted his head, his eyes glowed with Holy and righteous anger.

"We are under attack from those who would lead us. The world has always been dangerous to those who would dare to speak their beliefs. As Christians, we have been persecuted from the beginning. But now, we are about to return to the state we faced before Constantine converted. The government is now our enemy. We can wish it were not so, but wishes are best left to children."

The Bishop became the pacing lion, the general before his troops, the Holy Warrior, ready to lead against overwhelming odds. The men around him picked up his emotions.

"They have tied the hands of my priests. And believe me, any government so in love with paperwork as our friends in Prague has a list of every priest in the country. We make a show of obeying the laws here in the Cathedral. But you will not be so restricted. You will have no collars, no churches, no vestments. You will keep your jobs, your wives, your lives. But you will add this."

One man raised his hand. I couldn't see faces in the candlelight.

"How do we do this? How can we even be priests? I have two children at home, and another on the way."

"I can answer that only one way: let me worry about it. As a bishop, I have the authority to ordain priests. I choose to ignore certain rules and qualifications as I exercise my authority. Any problems that come of this will come to me. You are innocent of any wrongdoing."

Another man spoke.

"How are we supposed to be priests, though? Without a church, I mean."

"Do you think God is limited in where He can go? Does He only live in the house that Man built?"

"Well, no, I wouldn't presume…"

"Exactly. We presume many things in our Church, and few of those have any real basis. The first priests were not men of Holy Orders; they were married men, fathers, who lived their lives. Some were even women. They met in homes and fields and caves. Their churches were wherever faithful people gathered. Your churches will be the same. You will gather the faithful to you, in places of safety, to celebrate. You will baptize, marry, and bless those who ask."

"Will we be real priests?"

"Yes. In every sense of the word, you will be real priests, with the same authority as your friend Jan over there. The only difference is, you will have to hide that authority around anyone you cannot trust. But, before you leave here tonight, you will be priests, and not one person on Earth will be able to say different."

When I became a priest, I was aware of how many rules the Bishop broke and how many stages I did not go through. My ordination, though, was as close to normal as we could make it. For these men, everything was changed. The Bishop gave the right blessings, and I stood as witness and sponsor. But, overall, the entire ceremony consisted of the Bishop telling the men they had been ordained and them accepting his charge.

They were not entered on any roll; no official paperwork would exist. I had not considered my role in this enterprise beyond that of messenger between the Bishop and these hidden men. But I was something more: I was the record of their lives. I was the one who carried their stories, their names, their truths. The weight of this truth buckled my knees, and I knelt to pray for guidance.

We stayed in that dusty cellar all night, deep in prayer. In the morning, I arranged the days I would come to each and the signal they could use to summon me. The Bishop gave each man a breviary and a narrow, violet cord to use as a stole. These were the only outward signs of their vocations, and they were urged to hide them in a safe place.

They became warriors, alone in the world against an
unrelenting enemy, and I prayed for their safety.

16

I kept my dual role of parish priest and underground contact for three years. I would have stayed longer, but my parishioners died or moved away until there was no one left to join me for Mass. The young people did not return to fill the spaces, either scared of or aligned with the new communist government.

I was left without a job, but the Bishop found a way to occupy my time: I too went underground. I was not as well known in Brno as some priests, and the Bishop found a way to arrange paperwork to make it seem as if I had never finished my ordination. The irregularity of my priesthood worked to my advantage, as the Bishop had never gotten around to filling in all the proper paperwork after the war. We started a rumor about me abandoning my training over a woman, and I disappeared into the city.

I had the perfect cover. Vavrinec had decided to return to Brno and reopen his family's music store; I became his delivery driver. Behind the delivery crates, hidden in a toolbox, I kept everything I needed to turn the van into a mobile church.

I did most of my work outside of towns and cities. The countryside was dotted with small churches, built of old stone and held together by older families. It was remarkably easy to gather the people together for Mass. I simply had to park next to the church and someone would wander over from a field. I'd explain who I was and left the rest up to the locals. Children were dispatched and the families gathered after sunset. I never gave my full name. I was just "Father Jan," and that was enough for the people.

I did my best to avoid patterns. I would repeat visits, but never on the same day of the week, or in the same order, or even at regular intervals. I didn't even take the delivery van every time. I sewed several hidden pockets into the lining of the leather jacket I wore to protect me on my motorcycle, and I was able to carry everything I needed without any outward sign.

I was also able to look in on some of the underground priests as I traveled around the country. I had not seen Miklos in two years when I decided to visit. He was still at the hotel, which was in much better shape than my last visit. Miklos was still behind the front desk, but a bright-eyed girl joined him.

"And who is this little princess?"

"This is my daughter, Branka. Branka, this is my good friend Jan."

The girl had all of her fingers in her mouth as she studied me. I must have passed the test as she pulled out her fingers and waved her dripping hand at me. Miklos lifted her down from the counter and excused himself while he carried her up to Ana in the family apartment.

"She is beautiful, Miklos."

"Yes. She looks just like Ana. I have a photograph of her at that age. They are identical."

"You're a lucky man."

"Yes. Yes, I am. But you didn't come here to visit, did you?"

"Actually, I did."

"Really? I was sure you had been sent to reprimand me, or tell me I really am not a priest."

"Why would you think that?"

"I haven't been very successful here. I don't hold regular Mass, and I haven't even tried to get into the church."

"Why would you try to get into the church?"

"I thought we were supposed to take over the duties in empty churches."

"Not really. You're supposed to stay hidden, and holding Mass in a church here in town would be a little obvious."

"About all I've done is marry a couple of my friends and baptize Branka and a few other children."

"That is about all we were hoping for. Don't worry so much, Miklos. You're doing just fine."

"I keep feeling like I should be doing more."

"Like what?"

"Shouldn't we be speaking out against the government? Rallying the people together? Fighting back?"

"The country isn't ready for that yet. I think that's why the communists were able to take power so easily. Everyone is so tired of politics. If we start fighting back openly, we become the ones who are causing disruptions. Nobody wants disruptions; they just want peace."

"But they aren't going to get peace."

"I know that. But most people don't. The way they see it, the Soviets saved us from the Nazis, so the Soviet style of government cannot be all bad."

"Jan, I don't understand all this. I've been trying to figure out my role since I left Brno."

"You're already fulfilling your role better than you know. You're helping the people you can help; you're watching and listening. Information is the best weapon we have in this battle."

"I haven't learned much. About all I know is to keep my head down. I don't want to end up like my friend, Havel. He spoke up in a city council meeting and was arrested the next day."

"What happened to him?"

"He was gone for months. When he came back, he looked like he'd aged decades. Now he cannot even go outside without being followed."

"That poor man. Does he have any family?"

"Not anymore. His parents died years ago, and the Nazis sent his wife to Poland. She didn't come back."

"Where is he?"

"His house had been emptied and sold while he was gone, so I'm letting him stay in the hotel. He's upstairs right now."

"Do you think he would like to leave?"

"I think he would leave in a minute if he could. But I said, he's followed."

"He is, but I'm not."

"What are you going to do? Slip him out on the back of your motorcycle?"

"I didn't bring my motorcycle this time. I have a van. It's parked a few blocks from here."

"A few blocks is a few blocks too far."

I looked around the lobby. In one corner sat an old upright piano.

"I don't suppose that piano needs tuning."

"The piano? I don't think it even works anymore."

We walked over to the piano. I pressed one of the keys, but nothing happened. The lid had not been opened in a long time, so Miklos helped me swing it open. Inside was a nest of broken wires and cracked wooden hammers. The whole thing was nothing more than a fancy box of worthless debris.

"This is perfect. Help me pull out all these wires."

Miklos brought out two pairs of pliers and we swiftly stripped out the mess. When we finished, we went up to the room where Havel hid. Miklos tapped the door in a strange pattern and the door opened slowly.

"Havel? I've brought someone to see you."

The man who emerged from behind the door moved with the exaggerated gait of the very old or the very sick. His eyes had dark circles under them, and his skin was a color that reminded me of the miners I'd known, pale from a complete lack of sun exposure.

"Who is he? Is he from the government?"

"No, Havel. He's like me."

"He runs a hotel?"

"No. The other job."

"Oh. OH! You're a ..."

I nodded.

"No offense, sir, but what good is another priest?"

"Under normal circumstances, not much. But I happen to have something I doubt any other priest has."

"And what is that?"

"I have a delivery van."

Havel stared at me for several moments, then burst out laughing.

"A delivery van? What am I supposed to do with a delivery van?"

"You're supposed to hide in it and let me take you away from here."

Havel's eyes slowly lit with a tiny glimmer of hope.

"Away?"

"Yes. First to Brno. Maybe out of the country from there."

"Impossible. The borders are all closed."

"I didn't say it would be easy. But the first step is to get you out of here. Are you willing to come?"

The man sat on the bed for several minutes with his eyes closed.

"Yes. I will come. But how are you going to get me out of here? I cannot leave without being watched."

"Well, Miklos and I have figured something out that, we think, will get you out of here without anyone seeing anything."

I explained about the piano and my job as a delivery driver for a musical instrument shop. Havel quickly agreed and was eager to leave. I left him and Miklos as they went through his few possessions. He could not take much. I went back to where I had left the van and changed into my work overalls. I pulled my cap low over my eyes as I pulled up to the front door, and I brought in a large order pad. I filled out the order to make it look like Vavrinec had been contacted weeks ago to pick up and rebuild the piano.

Havel came down the stairs in a tattered suit, with a small bag in his hands. We put the bag in first, and then helped Havel climb into the piano. We were lucky he was so thin. The piano was on wheels, so Miklos and I just wheeled it down the boards I kept in the back of the van for real deliveries. When the piano was safely strapped into the back, I shook Miklos's hand and left, just another worker about his business.

I waited until I was far out of town and nobody was in sight on the road before I let Havel out of the piano. He rode the rest of the way to Brno in the back, with a blanket nearby to pull over his head if we were stopped.

As we neared Brno, Havel climbed back into the piano. I drove through the streets toward Vavrinec's store. Every time I saw a group of young men standing together, I pulled my cap low over my eyes. I could not tell who was a Communist and who was just passing the time of day with friends.

When I pulled up to the shop's street, I saw two large automobiles parked in front. Few enough people owned autos, and fewer still owned such large and well cared for specimen; I became concerned. These had the look of government vehicles, as did the two largish men standing with their backs to Vavrinec's windows. I pulled into the alley behind the store where the van usually sat and stopped.

"Havel, there may be a problem. I need you to stay in there until I come for you. Do you understand?"

I listened, but did not hear anything. I crept to the back and lifted the lid of the piano. Havel met my eyes.

"Try not to be too long; this is not the most comfortable of beds."

I tried to give him a brave smile, but I do not think I managed it. I left the van and walked in the back door of the shop, loudly banging the door open. I could not see faces clearly in the dim light, but I knew there were two men other than Vavrinec in the store.

"I'm back, sir. I brought that piano you wanted. It's in terrible shape, but we should be able to repair it."

One of the shapes spoke with a deep, gravely voice.

"Who is that?"

Vavrinec faced me.

"My assistant. He's been on an errand for me."

The man grunted and gestured to the other man.

"Just remember our deal, Vavrinec."

"Of course."

I waited until the door closed behind the man and the autos pulled away from the street before I turned to Vavrinec.

"Who was that? Government?"

"That, my dear Jan, was the best friend we could possibly have in this world: a crooked politician."

"How can he be our friend?"

"It is much easier to hide certain…activities…if the person who is supposed to stop you works for you."

"That explains all those crates in the basement."

"That it does. I've got food, medicine, newspapers, books…pretty much anything the government doesn't want us to have. All I have to do is slip a few cases of brandy and chocolate to our friend and everything becomes smooth. How did your visit with your friend go?"

"Judge for yourself." I explained about Havel and how I brought him to Brno.

"Hiding in the…" Vavrinec hurried out the back door.

We wheeled the piano into the shop before we helped Havel climb out. While he stomped around to get feeling back in one leg, Vavrinec examined the piano.

"To be honest, I think I can repair this. All it really needs is a new set of wires."

I stared at him for a moment.

"Is that really important, Vavrinec? Shouldn't we be helping Havel?"

"Relax, Jan. Your friend is in good hands. With the help of those nice gentlemen who just left, Havel will be out of Czechoslovakia within a week."

"And how many cases of chocolate will that cost you?"

"Keep joking, my friend, but I have just the thing. Before you came in, our friend was bemoaning the fact that his wife could not longer find any French perfume. I just so happen to have a few bottles tucked away in a corner."

Havel had been wandering around the back of the store, stretching his back while we talked. When he heard Vavrinec's idea, he came back over to us.

"Do you really think that will work?"

"Oh, absolutely. You hear on the radio about how impenetrable the border is; in truth, it is a sieve. People come and go every day. With just a bit of careful planning, you shouldn't be in any danger."

While we waited, we changed how Havel looked, from a pale, frail, dark-haired man to a sunburned blonde. We could not change his build with only a few days, but several large meals eased the stoop of his shoulders.

Three days after Havel arrived, Vavrinec found an envelope shoved under the front door of the shop. Inside was a complete set of Austrian identification papers: a passport, a travel permit, and a letter of introduction from the Czechoslovakian ambassador to Austria. To me, everything looked authentic; the number of ribbons and signatures was very impressive.

I did not go with Havel and Vavrinec to the border. When he returned, Vavrinec refused to talk about anything. He closed the store and sent me to visit my family for a week. I did not mind the

opportunity to see my parents, but I worried for my friend.

17

While I was spending my time finding priests, Vavrinec had married and moved into the large space above his family's music store. His father renovated the space for the family when Vavrinec was the only child. He had grown up there. I visited often during Seminary, usually for a meal. One afternoon, a few weeks after we helped Havel, I stopped by to pick up an underground newspaper Vavrinec helped create. I barely arrived before I found myself up a ladder, curtains in hand, under the critical eye of his wife. Vavrinec mirrored me on another ladder.

"Up a little, Jan. You are too low."

"He's taller than me. I can't reach that far."

"That is no excuse!"

Vavrinec listened to us with an easy smile. We eventually reached his wife's acceptable height and hung the curtains. As we came down, she gathered the material to either side and tied it back so the late afternoon light could come in. Vavrinec poured beer into three glasses and brought them in from the kitchen. He and I sat while his wife arranged.

"We're going to need something a little less chancy, Jan. It's too dangerous to just try to walk up the road to the border guards. There are patrols now, and they're shooting people as they try to cross. If Havel hadn't had those papers, they would have shot him. I watched the whole thing. They kept him in their guardhouse for over an hour."

"They're shooting people?"

"I assumed so. I stayed pretty far back and watched them unload about a dozen bodies behind the guardhouse. They looked like they were covered in blood. I even managed to take pictures."

"Pictures? You don't have them here, do you?"

"They're safe, and if someone finds them, there's no way to connect them to me. That's not the problem. We need to find a way to spread those pictures around. Too many people think the communists are a benign party."

I picked up the newspaper I'd come for.

"What about this?"

"Impossible. I try to help out, but the people who run it are a bunch of kids. They're enthusiastic, but naïve. One of them tried to break into the Party Headquarters, thinking they wouldn't mind when he identified himself as a journalist. He's in prison now. There wasn't even a trial."

"So, what do you suggest?"

"How about your people? The ones whose names are in your little book."

I touched the pocket where I kept my list of underground priests. As the idea spread, some of the other bishops in Czechoslovakia had joined in and started their own cadre of underground priests. Since I had been in on the plan from the start, and because of my mobility, I had the task of keeping a record of these brave men. Only I had all their names, the towns where they worked, and the details of their ordinations. I kept the list with me at all times, in one of the hidden pockets in my motorcycle jacket.

"I don't want to put them in more danger."

"I wouldn't want them to keep the photos. They could simply distribute them and get the rumors started."

"Would that work?"

"You know how fast stories and rumors can spread. Even if the photos are destroyed, the stories will continue."

"Say this works; say we distribute the photos and people tell the stories. Then what?"

"Then, nothing. We cannot truly fight the government yet. All we can do is inform the population about what is really going on."

"Do you think they'll care?"

Vavrinec could not answer me.

18

I handed out the photographs. And, a few months later, I heard the stories of border killings come back around. Nobody was surprised. I couldn't help feeling disappointed when nothing really changed.

I adjusted to life underground. I continued my pose of making deliveries around the district, and did what I could to serve the people in Brno as well. I came up with several schemes to circumvent the rules and bring the Church to the people. Some worked, others didn't. My most effective ruse involved a walk to the river and feeding the ducks.

Or, rather, I appeared to feed the ducks. The reality was slightly different. On my walks to the park, I met any number of people. I greeted each person with a handshake and a bit of conversation. The handshake hid the fact that I gave each person a Host, and the conversation gave them the time they should make their way to the river. When I arrived at the river, I stood and tore pieces of bread and threw them into the water. While I did this, I said Mass in a whisper, and the people I met on my walk would slowly join me at the bank. Several brought fishing poles. When I ran out of bread, I scratched my head, and every person would place the Host in their mouth.

On other days, I visited homes. A quick visit would lead to lunch, and the hosts would gather family and friends together for an impromptu gathering. At those, I paid more attention to form and ritual, and would perform a wide variety of priestly duties through the afternoon. More than a few young couples married in their grandmother's sitting room.

It was as I left one of these gatherings that my life shifted forever. I regularly came to the Cathedral to update the Bishop with any news. As I walked up the hill towards the Cathedral, I saw several autos with official seals on the doors pull up to the main doors. I found an alley where I could watch but not be seen. Nothing happened for several minutes.

And then the doors all but exploded outward. Men held the Bishop's arms to his sides, and escorted him to the cars. He was not quiet. His roars of outrage were incoherent, animal. My mouth hung open with shock, and I forgot to hide myself, but the government men did not notice me. They bundled the Bishop into the back of one car and left.

I walked into the street. I was alone. Not even the usual spies at their posts remained. I entered the Cathedral and saw how the Communists had expressed themselves while arresting my bishop. I had always thought the pews were bolted to the floor. And at one time, they may have been. But someone had moved, thrown, several out of place. The main altar was undamaged, but the door in the Communion rail was ripped from its hinges and discarded. I heard a moan and found one of the Cathedral priests against the wall, nursing a cut on his forehead.

"Father? Can you tell me what happened?"

"I … I don't know. I was polishing the rail when I heard someone run up behind me. I turned around and then everything went dark."

"It's ok, Father. Don't move. I need to see if anyone else is hurt. Are you alright to stay here by yourself?"

"I think so. Go and see, son. Don't worry about me."

I ran through the halls towards the Bishop's office. I didn't see anyone until I came to his door. Outside his office, a novice, undersized and away from home for the first time, bundled himself on the floor and wept. I grabbed his arms and lifted him to his feet.

"What happened? Where are they taking the Bishop?"

"They . . . I . . . they took him."

His eyes did not focus on me. I stood him against the wall and slapped his cheeks until he looked at me.

"We don't have time for that. Tell me what happened."

"I was coming down the hall with his coffee. I heard shouting. Something about a list. Then they pulled him out of the door and shoved him down the hall. They knocked me over. I spilled the coffee on the rug. I have to get the coffee out of the rug!"

"It's ok. Don't worry about the rug. Look at me. Talk to me. Did they say where they were taking him?"

"No . . . yes . . . Party headquarters. They said they were going to party headquarters."

"Damn. Did they say anything else?"

"I don't know. All I heard was yelling about a list."

I patted my jacket pocket. The only list I could think of was the one I carried at all times; the list of underground priests. They had the wrong man.

I sent the novice back to the kitchen. He still shook, but he was able to walk. I left him in the care of one of the brothers. I brought one of the other kitchen workers with me to the Cathedral, and we were able to bring the injured priest over to the residence. A novice was dispatched for a doctor, and I left. There was nothing more I could do.

19

Someone had talked.

It was as simple as that. I had a list of fifty-three names. Those fifty-three men each had friends and families who knew what they were doing. As they worked, they came in contact with hundreds of other people. And all of those people had friends and families. Our operation could not be kept secret. I had no doubt the government knew there were secret priests among the population. But someone needed to talk for them to make any sort of move.

I did not worry that the Bishop might give away any secrets. He was much stronger than they could understand, and I truly believed he would happily die if it would keep the rest of us safe. That was the only reason I did not immediately destroy my list or try to escape the country. But I did take a few precautions.

At the back of Vavrinec's shop was a wide wood staircase that led up to the storage loft, then to the apartment. With Vavrinec's help, I pried up two of the steps and attached a hinge. From the outside, they looked like normal risers. But, with a little tug, they slid out far enough to turn on the hinge to create a space large enough for me to slide through. I could lock the steps from the inside, to further confound any search attempts. Under the stairs, and between the supports, we created a comfortable, if tight, space where someone could hide for several days. We even stocked some canned food and a large canteen of water, just in case. Vavrinec fashioned a crude hammock out of some canvas sheets, and it was ready. His wife delighted in teasing me about the "priest hole," a term she picked up from reading British detective novels. I put a few other items I would need in my old satchel and kept it in the space: my old stole, a spare emergency-priest kit, an envelope full of money, my list of underground priests, and a loaded pistol.

I continued with my duties, and visited several of the underground priests. None of them could imagine anyone who might betray them. I advised them to create a false name to use while working. I could not see everyone, but each one promised to try to find out where the breach occurred.

On a late night in April, I returned from one of my trips. I was worried, as the priest I intended to visit had disappeared. I did not know if he had been arrested or had gone into hiding. I hoped for the latter.

I parked my motorcycle behind the music shop and climbed the fire escape to the apartment. I knew I could scrounge a meal from Vavrinec. I came in through the window and saw they had a visitor. I started to excuse myself for intruding when the visitor turned around.

It was Ana, Miklos's wife.

Her eyes were red and puffy from crying, and she had a handkerchief in her hands that she had twisted into a lace licorice stick. She stood when she saw me, then came over and wrapped her arms around me and wept.

I wasn't sure what to do. I had only met Ana a handful of times. Usually, when I visited Miklos, I met him away from the hotel, to avoid a pattern. I gave her a quick hug, then stepped back from her. It was only then I noticed she was very pregnant.

"Ana? What's going on? Where's Miklos?"

"Russia. He's in Russia."

"What?"

"The police came for him a month ago. They had one of those photographs you gave Miklos to pass around. They threatened me and Branka. They threatened my baby!"

She put her hand protectively on her swollen stomach.

"Ana, where's Branka? Did they take her somewhere?"

Vavrinec came over to us.

"She's in with our children, poor thing. She was exhausted when they got here."

"How did you know to come here?"

"Miklos told me all about the friend you had who owned a music store. And I remembered the name from your van when you helped move poor Havel. I saw from our window."

"Are you sure Miklos is in Russia?"

"Yes. They came and told me they were sending him to prison in Siberia. Why would they do that? Why send him so far away?"

Vavrinec answered.

"Because Russia is where all the real decisions are made. We can pretend we have our own government, but it is all a fairy tale, to keep the people happy."

I turned back to Ana.

"Do you know what Miklos told them?"

"Everything. About being a priest. About you. About the Bishop. They threatened Branka and me."

Ana grabbed my arm.

"That means they know who you are. And if they know who you are, they will figure out where you are ..."

Vavrinec went over to the front window and looked out.

"There are two cars and a panel truck across the street. I can see the glow from their cigarettes."

Vavrinec and I looked at each other.

"The priest-hole. You have to hide, Jan."

"What about them?"

I nodded to Ana, and included Branka in the question. Vavrinec thought for a moment.

"They probably followed you here, Ana. And I'm sure they know Jan is my friend. So, we'll tell the truth, up to a point. You came here looking for Jan. We'll say we haven't seen him for a few days, and don't know when he'll be back."

I nodded. It was the best we could do. I gave Vavrinec's wife a quick hug, then went with Vavrinec to the staircase. We had just opened the hidden door when someone started banging on the front door of the shop. Vavrinec and I looked at each other and he nodded

to me. He would do what had to be done to keep Ana and the kids

safe. My job was to survive. I climbed down and watched as the

door closed. I slid the bolt into place with a snap.

20

I couldn't hear anything in the space, other than footsteps on the stairs. I didn't dare light one of the candles I had with me, so I could not see my watch. I had no idea how long I stayed in that space. I only know it was long enough for me to sleep for several hours on the hammock. The "all clear" knock woke me.

I opened the door and squinted into the morning light that came through the windows. Vavrinec helped me out of the space.

"They're gone. They asked questions and threatened all of us, but we didn't tell them anything."

"Are they still watching?"

"One of the cars is still out front, and the other is at one end of the alley."

"So, what do we do now?"

"We get you out of here, that's what."

"And how do you propose we do that?"

"Do you really think I would bring my family here and not have an escape route?"

I smiled at him.

"Of course not. Don't know what I was thinking."

We went back to the apartment where the women had a large breakfast ready for everyone. The children sensed something was wrong and were as subdued as I had ever seen them. They barely remembered to fight with each other over who got which egg. We ate quickly and I gave each child a hug and a blessing before we left.

Vavrinec led me to the roof of the building and showed me his escape route. The buildings in that part of the city were built close together, and the roofs were a road. We jumped over the short walls between buildings and wove between chimneys. Two buildings down from the shop, Vavrinec had stored several boards that were long enough to reach across the alley to a building owned by a friend of his father's. We slid the boards across and he gave me the key to the roof door. I had my satchel under my jacket and a hat pulled low over my eyes. Vavrinec promised he would get my motorcycle to me in a park where we had gone many times. We would not meet in the park.

I started to shake his hand, then switched to a hug. Vavrinec was my best friend.

I crawled across the boards and had the door open by the time Vavrinec pulled the boards back to his side of the space. I walked down the stairs and out the front door and joined the people on the street.

The park was several kilometers away, and I took every precaution I could think of to confuse anyone who might follow me. I walked in the opposite direction, then rode a bus across town, still far from my destination. I ducked through the back doors of shops and walked down alleyways behind buildings. I joined any crowd I could find, and took off or put on my jacket and cap every few minutes. Several hours later, I found myself at the entrance to the park. I could see my motorcycle parked at the curb, and thought I saw Vavrinec in the distance, fishing pole in hand. I did not see either car that had been parked outside of the shop the night before.

I checked the tank: full. I silently thanked Vavrinec as I started the bike and rode into traffic. I looked back, but could not see him. I took the closest route out of town and drove for several hours before I turned toward the border.

The trip to the Austrian border took me the rest of the day. I did not want to drive at night. If I used my headlight, someone might see, and if I didn't, a small rock on the road could spell disaster. I pulled into a thick copse of trees and hid the motorcycle with a few branches. I did not try to start a fire. Instead, I sat with my back to a tree and the pistol in my hand. I did not want to shoot anyone; I didn't know if I would be able to if the need arose.

With the dawn came the rumble of heavy vehicles. I made sure I was well hidden and watched as several military trucks come down the road. The first two had young troops, while the rest looked like they carried building material. It wasn't until the last trucks passed that I figured out what they were building: a fence. The final trucks held coil after coil of sharpened wire, similar to what I had seen back in Nikde around the prisoner camp. They were turning the whole country into a prison camp.

I knew I was near the border. A few kilometers and I would be in Austria. But I could not just ride down the road and cross over. I remembered those photographs. And that was before they decided to encircle the nation. With the added troops, crossing on the road would be nearly impossible.

I pushed my bike deeper into the trees and looked for any sort of path that might lead me in the right direction. I could have abandoned the motorcycle, but if I found an open area, I could move much faster than troops on foot. It took me nearly as long to cross

those last few kilometers to the border as it had taken me to drive
from Brno the day before.

I found a narrow valley, a jagged cut between two low
mountains, bisected by a slow stream. The tree line stood well back
from the water, as most of the ground was covered with small, pink
boulders. Across the stream, scraggly pines replaced the beech trees
I'd been riding through. I knew the border was very close. I was
fairly sure I could see Austria from where I was.

I turned over the engine and idled for a moment while I
looked over possible routes. An old cattle path followed the creek in
the direction I needed to go. I started slow, ready to jump off if I
needed to.

At the end of the valley, I saw a wide swath that had been
recently cleared of trees, the stumps cut close to the ground. I
stopped just short of crossing the area. It almost looked like a new
road would be built there, and I even saw some deep tire ruts. Then it
came to me: this was where the fence would go up. I had found the
border. I gunned the engine and started across.

Just as I came into the open, I saw the truck convoy from the
road. The troops had unloaded the material and were busy digging

postholes and stringing wires. A shout went up when they saw me, and several men grabbed for rifles. I sped up and was nearly to the tree line when they opened fire. Several bullets passed close over my head, but I did not slow down. I ducked between two trees and was gone.

I drove for hours before an Austrian patrol found me. They took the pistol from me and gave me a heel of bread and some sausage to eat. I hadn't spoken German since the war, but I was able to make them understand I needed to see someone with authority. They placed my motorcycle in the back of a truck and drove me to an encampment.

Inside the camp, row upon row of canvas tents had been erected, creating a whole city. The soldiers unloaded my motorcycle and pointed me toward the command post. As I pushed my machine along the rutted path through the middle of the camp, I realized that everyone around me was speaking Czech. I started to play closer attention to the people; some bore minor wounds while others looked exhausted, but all were my countrymen.

The command post of the camp was just another tent, although it was ten times larger than any of the others. A line of people, refugees, stretched out from the open flap, and most of the people sat on the ground. The man at the end sat propped up on his elbows, his legs stretched in front of him. As I walked up, he lifted the brim of his cap enough to see me.

"You wouldn't have any food, would you?"

I looked at him; he did not seem to be starving, or even uncomfortable.

"No. Don't they have enough food for everyone here?"

"Oh, yes. But I've been in line all morning, and I'd hate to lose my place."

He replaced his cap and seemed to go to sleep. I pushed my motorcycle under a nearby tree and sat down. With this many refugees, the authorities had to know about the deaths at the border. I felt the packet of pictures in my pocket. In Brno, I could have died because of them; here, they might not even matter.

As I sat, I saw a tall, thin man walking down the row of waiting people. I had to blink my eyes several times before I believed what I saw: he wore the cassock of a priest! I stood and abandoned my motorcycle under the tree. I ran up to him and grabbed at his sleeve. He smiled at me and spoke in German accented Czech.

"Easy, my son. You are safe here. Have they shown you where you can sleep? Are you hungry?"

I could not answer. I tried, my mouth moving, but no words came out. The priest looked distressed and led me back under the tree where I'd been sitting.

"Please sit down out of the sun. Are you alright?"

I cleared my throat and wiped my eyes, where tears had come up. Finally, I managed to speak.

"My name is Jan Svestka, and I am a priest."

Made in the USA
Las Vegas, NV
28 November 2021